Mob Ties 2
Code of Silence

Lock Down Publications and Ca$h
Presents

MOB TIES 2

A Novel by *SAYNOMORE*

Lock Down Publications

P.O. Box 944
Stockbridge, Ga 30281
www.lockdownpublications.com

Lock Down Publications
Like our page on Facebook: Lock Down Publications
@
www.facebook.com/lockdownpublications.ldp
Cover design and layout by: **Dynasty Cover Me**
Book interior design by: **Shawn Walker**
Edited by: **Leondra Williams**

Stay Connected with Us!

Text **LOCKDOWN** to 22828 to stay up-to-date with
new releases, sneak peaks, contests and more…
Thank you!

Submission Guideline.

Submit the first three chapters of your completed manuscript to ldpsubmissions@gmail.com, subject line: Your book's title. The manuscript must be in a .doc file and sent as an attachment. Document should be in Times New Roman, double spaced and in size 12 font. Also, provide your synopsis and full contact information. If sending multiple submissions, they must each be in a separate email.

Have a story but no way to send it electronically? You can still submit to LDP/Ca$h Presents. Send in the first three chapters, written or typed, of your completed manuscript to:

LDP: Submissions Dept
P.O. Box 944
Stockbridge, Ga 30281

DO NOT send original manuscript. Must be a duplicate.

Provide your synopsis and a cover letter containing your full contact information.

Thanks for considering LDP and Ca$h Presents.

SAYNOMORE

First and foremost, I want to thank God Almighty and my Lord and Savior Jesus Christ for the many blessings He had given me. I also want to thank big bro, Ca$h, for giving me the opportunity to fulfill my dream of becoming a published author.

A truly big thank you to everyone associated with Lock Down Publications from the editors to the highest-ranking members of the staff. Thanks for working so diligently on my project. Much love to all of you.

A regular citizen who reports seeing a crime isn't a snitch or a rat. The criminals were just sloppy. Snitches and rats aren't the same thing. A snitch is someone minding folk's business to find information they can sell for a prize or trade for some other form of compensation.

A rat is a traitor, a deceiver, planner or physical participator. He doesn't sell secrets for power or cash. He betrays the trust of his team or his family hoping to save his own cowardly ass. The difference is at least a snitch is human, but a rat is a "Fucking Rat Period"!!!

- Morgan Freeman

SAYNOMORE

Prologue

I can't believe this shit. People get killed every fucking day and you got this witness telling what she seen all over the damn news. Ain't no difference between a fucking snitch and a witness. They need to be laying somewhere dead letting the fucking rats eat away at their rotten corps, said Frankie talking to himself as he smoked his cigar and drinking his coffee watching the morning news. He couldn't believe what he was hearing so he turned up the TV to make sure what he was hearing was right.

"This is Barbara Smith, we just got Breaking News a little over an hour ago. New Jersey Police got a tip on a big shipment of cocaine that was to arrive at Port Newton. Four men were arrested, and two tons of cocaine was seized by the Coast Guard." Frankie's eyes were glued to the TV, that was his shipment.

"Son of a bitch. Where are my keys?" Grabbing the keys off the nightstand and running out the door.

"Mr. Landon, is everything alright?"

"Ms. Simpson call Marcus and tell him to meet me at the docks in New Jersey right now," Frankie stated as he opened his car door to get in.

"God damn the car won't start." He began to kick the car, and punching the steering-wheel as he kept on turning the key to try to get the car started.

"Mr. Landon?"

"Ms. Simpson, What I ask you to do? I ain't say come to the car, I said call Marcus."

"I know what you said, Mr. Landon."

"So then why are you still standing here?"\ Do as you was told," he said yelling as he opened the car door to get out.

Stopping in his tracks looking at Ms. Simpson, "You got to be fucking kidding me. They sent you? At least give me the respect and tell me who paid you to do it. I took care of you for seven years and you pull a gun on me?"

"Some things don't need to be talked about Frankie. But I will tell you this, I was the one who called and dropped the tip on your shipment and took the battery cable a loose on your car."

Looking at the gun pointed at him thinking how if he had the chance, her fucking throat would be cut from ear to ear.

"Just make sure they bury me shallow bitch. I'll see your ass on the other side."

"No, you won't," as sparks fired as bullets wrapped through Frankie's chest dropping him to his knees.

"Breathe, Frankie. That was only four shots to your chest."

Blood was coming from his mouth as he was looking up at Ms. Simpson. As he fell forward, she let off two more shots to Frankie's back watching his body jump as he took a deep breath, walking away with the snub nose .38 in her hand. Laying in a pool of blood all Frankie could see was a blurry figure of Ms. Simpson walking away.

Chapter One

"Mrs. LaCross, you have a phone call on line one."

"Kim, will you inform them that I will call them back. I'm in a meeting right now."

"I told them that but they said it was urgent."

"Here I come now. Will y'all please excuse me? I need to take this call," said Jamila walking out of the conference room. Entering her office, she picked up the phone. "Hello, this is Ms. LaCross."

"Hey Jamila, this is Marcus. I'm sorry to pull you out of your meeting."

"Oh, Hi Marcus. No problem. What can I do for you?"

"Did you see the news this morning?"

"Yea, I was going to call Frankie and ask him about that."

"Well, that's not the bad news. That's just the tip of the iceberg, Jamila."

"What is *that*?" asked Jamila.

"Frankie was shot six times this morning at his house. We ain't find him until about a half hour after he was shot. He lost a lot of blood. They don't know if he's going to make it or not. He's in ICU and he's very weak, but he asked to see you. Let me forewarn you, there are a lot of police and news teams up there."

"Marcus don't worry about that. Let him know I'll be there sometime today."

"I'll let him know."

Jamila laid her hands on the desk after hanging up the phone asking herself, "Who could have got close enough to Frankie to have shot him at his house? And who would want him dead?" Walking back in the meeting, "I'm so sorry everyone but something very important just came up that's needs my attention. It's very urgent."

"Lorenzo, do you mind handling all the details and going over the stuff we are asking for?"

"Sure, I can take it from here Jamila."

"I'm sorry again, but I do have an emergency to take care of right away."

"Don't worry, Jamila. I can take care of things from here."

"Thank you, Lorenzo,"

Walking out of Jelani's, Jamila walked across the street to the flower shop.

"James!"

"Hello, Ms. LaCross. Let me guess something red and white roses?"

"Yes James."

"You must have really lost somebody close because I know I will see your face every week."

"James, loyalty don't stop when you stop breathing. True loyalty is forever and a day. Take care."

"You too, Ms. LaCross!"

Within twenty minutes Jamila pulled up at the cemetery as she does every week. She laid the white roses down next to Isaiah's grave and the red roses next to Nayana's grave. The white roses were for the innocent and the red roses for the blood she spilled. After a few minutes she said the Lord's Prayer. When she was finished, she said Rest in Peace, I love you. As she was leaving it started to rain. Once in the car she called a detective friend of hers.

"Hello, Mario. This is Jamila. How are you doing today?"

"I'm good Jamila, how you been?"

"I could be better. Listen, I'm calling because I need a favor."

"What can I do for you?"

"So, I'm taking it you heard about Frankie?"

"Yea, I just found out about two hours ago. "

"Well, I need your help to get in there to see him."

"Whoa, now that's a tough one Jamila."

"I know Mario but, I need to get in there without the cameras and police seeing me visit a crime boss."

"Look, I have an idea, dress up like a detective. I have an extra badge and belt. And we're going to say you are a detective from Jersey here to talk to Mr. Landon. And you might not be noticed by the police or news cameras up there."

"Ok. I'll be there by 7:30 tonight. I'll call you when I'm out front."

"I'll be waiting Jamila."

"Thank you, Mario."

"You're welcome."

"Let me call Lorenzo and I'll call you back when I'm out front."

"I'll be waiting on your call."

"Hello?"

"Lorenzo."

"Jamila, what's going on? Is everything alright?"

"No, Frankie's been shot six times. I'm on my way to go see him now at the hospital."

"Do they know who shot him?" asked Lorenzo.

"No, not yet but it happened at his house this morning. So, it had to be someone close to him. It was this morning before Marcus was there."

"Damn, well I made the deal with the first Bank of America."

"That's great!" I'm sorry I had to leave."

"Well, that's what you got me for."

"You're right. I will call you when I leave the hospital."

"Let me know if you need me Jamila."

"I will."

SAYNOMORE

Chapter Two

Making it to her house, Jamila put on some honey brown pants with a black shirt, black shoes and a honey brown trench coat with matching hat. Her hair was covered over her face. If you ain't know no better, you would have thought she was a real detective. Pulling up to the hospital she said to herself, "let me call Mario and tell him I'm out here in the front."

"Hey Mario, it's Jamila. I'm out front."

"I see you, I'm on my way out front now to you. I'm in the lobby. I see you took it to the extreme with the hat and coat. You could have fooled the shit out of me if I ain't know who you were."

"I tried. You know I have an image to uphold now.

"Listen to me Jamila, I can only give you ten to fifteen minutes at the most. Now I'm giving you a heads up. His attorney never left his side and he's still in there right now."

"I got this, I'm ready Mario."

"Look to the left, you see all of them cameras up over there?"

"Yea, I have never seen so many cameras up here before like this."

"I told you there is a lot of media over this right now and a lot of public figures involved in this as well. They don't want a war to start like the last one over this like the Lenacci family four years ago."

"I understand."

As Jamila made it to Frankie's floor, she saw police officers posted up at Frankie's door.

"Police at his door, Mario?"

"I told you this is big, Jamila. A crime boss shot down at his house and a tip on his shipment is headline news."

"Hey Wright!"

"Mario, what's up? It's been a while. How you been?"

"Good just cleaning up the bullshit in these streets. This is Detective Cheryl from the 26th Precinct in New Jersey here to see Mr. Landon."

"Nice to meet you Detective Cheryl."

"Likewise, Jason. Is Mr. Landon inside?"

"Yes, he is with his attorney."

"Ok, I'll just be a few minutes." Jamila opened the door.

"Mr. Landon, I'm Detective Cheryl from the 26th Precinct in New Jersey here to ask you some questions."

"My client is in no condition to talk."

"Shhh, it's me Jamila, Mr. Russo."

"How did you get in here?" asked Russo.

"I have my ways and its Detective Cheryl." Mr. Russo just shook his head at her and smiled.

Walking to Frankie's bed, Jamila touched his hand. Frankie looked up at her and coughed two times.

"I knew you would come."

"Do you want me to get you some water?"

"No, I'm fine but I need you."

"Frankie, who did this to you?"

"Ms. Simpson shot me, and she also called New Jersey and gave them the tip on my shipment."

"Why did she do this?"

"I don't know. She thought she killed me but listen, this is what I need you to do for me. I need you to take my place until I get out the hospital."

"Frankie, why me and not Marcus?"

"He has a lot to learn. He's not ready to run my family."

"Ok, I will try Frankie."

"Jamila, I trust you."

"Jamila."

"Yes, Mr. Russo."

" I will contact you tomorrow and go over all the final details with you."

"Ok, I will be waiting on your call."

At that point Detective Mario opened up the door.

"Cheryl, it's time."

"Ok, here I come now."

Taking Mr. Russo's card, "I will be in touch Mr. Russo."

"I will talk to you soon Detective Cheryl," walking out the door.

"Jason, you have a good night."

"You too detective."

Walking down the hallway, "Mario where are all the cameras and news teams at?"

"They realized that standing around was pointless. They left, no one would give them the answers to their questions."

"Jamila, I have to go see the Captain. You good from here?"

"Yea, I can make it out of here now. Thanks Mario."

"No problem."

When she made it out front of the hospital it was raining, and no one was insight. It was dark outside she kept on hearing footsteps but when she turned around no one was insight. Then she heard a voice, "excuse me detective, detective."

When she turned around to see who was calling her, she saw two armed men with their guns pointed at her. She took off running behind a car pulling her gun out. She got up and looked at them and shot three times hitting a parked car's windshield.

"Go that way. She's behind that car."

Looking for a place to run a black SUV pulled up and two more men jumped out with masks over their face with guns in their hand. "Where she at?"

Jamila got up and started running through the parking lot as they were shooting at her. That's when she saw Mario getting in the SUV with one of the guys. She knew then he set her up. She saw one of the guys running towards her. Once he was close enough, she shot him in the face dropping him. Two more men jumped out another truck. That's when you heard two officers running out the hospital yelling, "Freeze" as they started shooting at them.

Jamila was ducked down behind the car when she heard police sirens coming closer. She saw the truck Mario jumped in speeding through the parking lot. She started shooting at the driver's window making the driver turn hitting a parked car flipping the truck over. She ran to the side of the truck as the police was pulling into the parking lot. One of the men was hanging outside the truck window as Jamila walked up to him.

"Now look at you. You tried to kill me but now you are laying here. Let's see the face behind the mask." When she reached down and pulled his mask off, she saw it was Mario, looking at his face.

Jamila listened.

"No fuck you," as she pointed her gun at his face.

"Don't, don't Jamila."

Putting her gun to his head she shot him two times in the face, killing him. She looked around and saw two more officers laid out who was shot. There was a black Hummer across the street. Its occupants were watching everything and when they saw Mario get killed, they pulled off.

Jamila made it to the other side of the parking lot and made her way down the street without being seen. She knew someone was out to kill her and Frankie, but *who* was the question. She pulled out her phone and called Lorenzo, who answered in the third ring.

"Lorenzo?" she uttered.

"Hey, what's up Jamila? Why you out of breath?"

"Someone just tried to kill me."

"What, where you at?" asked Lorenzo.

Walking down straight path from hospital. "I need you to pick me up."

"I'm coming now. Where's your car at?"

"I had to leave it at the hospital, too many police up there."

"Ok, I'm on my way to you. I'll be there in ten minutes the most.

*****

"Detective Boatman, what the fuck happened out here?"

"Cheif, we don't know yet. All we know is that we have nine dead bodies and three of them are officers that came to the scene. One is Detective Mario and five John Doe's at this point until we can identify them."

"It looks like World War III out here. A truck flipped over with three dead bodies inside. Dead bodies over there. Shit."

"Yea, and I got some more fucked up news for you. Come take a look at this over here."

"And what's over there, Boatman?"

"Detective Mario was with whoever these guys where he was one of them."

"Fuck me. That's all we need is for this to get out to the fucking press, that one of our very own New York finest is mixed up in this bullshit. You there, tape this shit up and I don't want no news teams on my crime scene."

*****

"Jamila, tell me what happened now."

"Lorenzo, my mind is racing fast. Frankie's shipment gets tipped off by Ms. Simpson, then she shoots him. Then someone tries to have me killed. I don't know what the fuck is going on right now or what my next move is going to be. I need to call the other families and try and pick up on their vibes."

"So, when you want to make these calls?"

"In a few days. Let's see who reaches out to me first. And I also might have a meeting in a few days with Frankie's attorney."

"About what?" asked Lorenzo.

"I'm taking over the Landon family for a little while until Frankie is out the hospital. So, I'll need you to handle all business affairs with our family. I'm going to call a family meeting about that."

"Are you still in contact with your underground friends in New Jersey?"

"Do you mean my underground friends or my politician friends?"

"Everything we do I want to be underground until we find out who is behind all of this."

"Yea, I still have a few underground connects."

"Ok, see if you can find out where they moved Frankie's drugs to and who is running the case for me."

"Jamila what you got in mind?"

"I don't know yet Lorenzo."

Chapter Three

The Next Day…

"Officer Wright, come in and have a seat. So how are you doing today?"

"I'm fine Chief Tadem."

"I called you in here because I need to ask you a few questions."

"Ok Sir."

"I went over the video tapes on the floor you were on last night to see everyone who visited Mr. Landon last night. And I'm trying to find out who was the lady who was with Detective Mario. We never saw her face not one time in the surveillance videos. But we saw you shake hands with her." So, can you tell me who she is?"

"That was my first time meeting her, but Detective Mario told me she was a detective from New Jersey here to ask Mr. Landon some questions. She told me her name was Cheryl. I've never seen her until yesterday. But his attorney was in there with them also."

"I know I talked with him and he told me the same thing and I called New Jersey. They never heard of her a Detective Cheryl at all. Thanks for coming by officer."

"No problem sir."

"Who the fuck is our mystery girl? And what did she want with Frankie?" Chief Tadem asked himself. Picking up his office phone he called Detective Boatman.

"Detective Boatman."

"It's me," Chief Tadem stated, "Listen up. I need you to find out who this damn female is who went and saw Frankie Landon last night, before the shoot out in the parking lot."

"Ok, Sir I'm on it. I won't let you down sir."

"I know you won't."

Hanging up the phone Chief Tadem said to himself, "this just keeps getting worse and worse. What the fuck is happening to my city?"

*****

"Mr. Russo, you have a Jamila LaCross here to see you."

"Send her in please."

"He said you can go on back Ms. LaCross."

"Thank you."

"You're welcome."

"Hello Mr. Russo. How are you feeling today?"

"I'm good for the most part. How is Frankie doing?"

"I had him moved to a private part of the hospital so he can rest."

"That's good."

"I heard you had a hard time leaving the hospital last night."

"Yea, I did, but I'm here and they are not."

"And that's a true statement Jamila."

"Well Jamila, Chief Tadem contacted me this morning. They are trying to find out who you are. I told them all I know you are a Detective from Jersey so I'm just giving you a head's up."

"Thank you."

"So, here are the papers Frankie wanted me to give to you to sign. He is giving you 49% of his business and if he dies you will get the other 51% of his business. I need you to sign these right here Ms. LaCross."

"And what am I signing?"

"These papers just say if anything was to happen to Mr. Landon you will take full ownership of his establishments."

"Does he owe any banks for anything?"

"Yes, he owes $2.5 million to untie trust."

"What is his net worth?" asked Jamila.

"From all his businesses?"

"It comes up to $100,000,000. Jamila, Frankie trusts you."

"I know, but I don't understand why me?"

"Because he thinks it's someone from his own family who set it up and he might be right."

"Are all these the papers I needed to sign?"

"Yes, that's it."

"Ok, Mr. Russo I will be in touch you have a nice day."

"One more thing Jamila before you go?"

"Yes?"

"I work for you now. This law firm is owned by Frankie."

Jamila nodded her head as she walked out the door, she pulled out her phone and called Lorenzo.

"Hey, what's up Jamila?"

"We need to talk. Meet me at the Waste Plant in fifteen minutes."

"I'll be there."

"I have my own family to run and keep in line and five companies to run. Now I have Frankie's family and companies to run too. And someone out here is trying to kill me," said Jamila to herself. As she pulled up at the Waste Plant, Lorenzo was pulling up at the same time she was. Lorenzo walked up and got in her car.

"What's up Jamila?"

"I just left Frankie's attorney's office and I own all of his companies as of right now. I even have his family to look out after right now also."

"Jamila, four years ago you took on the most powerful family in New York and won. We lost a few good family members but, you made a way for us. Now every family in New York knows who you are, and they respect you. And they know who runs Queens. Your hands are in every politician's pocket so you just have to think like you did before."

"You know what Lorenzo, call all the families and set up a meeting with everyone. And ask them will they have a sit down with us next week Monday at 1 p.m. To let them know what's going on with Frankie and to handle all of his business affairs."

"Ok. I will. And I have a few guys working on the drugs that were seized."

"And how is that going?"

"I will know something tonight. Do you think it might be the Lenacci family again, Jamila?"

"I don't know, but if so, why Frankie and not me?"

"You have to ask yourself that question Lorenzo, if you're going to think like that. Me and Vinnie are doing a lot of good business together and I don't think he wants to ruin that relationship."

"So, did you agree to help them cleanup they money?"

"Lorenzo, four powerful men was killed in that family by our hands. Three we did and one we set up without even knowing about it. So, when he came to me, I shook his hand. Plus, he helped us kill Alex."

"So which establishments are we cleaning the money through?"

"That's not important, but for every million we get $300,000. We just got to keep moving like we are and stay low, so we don't have to worry about the FEDS."

"So how is Marcus taking the news?"

"I haven't talked to him yet, so I don't know. I just hope he respects Frankie's decision. Well, I have another meeting with first Bank of America about the Waste Plant. Fabio was renting the building but I'm trying to get them to sell it to us."

"How much are they trying to sell for?" asked Jamila.

"$3.5 million, but I'm trying to talk them down to $3 million no more than $3.2 million."

"Ok, let me know how it goes. I have a meeting with a few people within the next hour, so I'll see you back at the restaurant."

"Who are you having a meeting with?"

"Two DA's and a judge. I'm trying to get them in my pockets too."

"So how is that going?"

"Not so good but, it's a work in progress. So, let me go and you go take care of your business and we will meet up later."

*****

"Jason Scott, looking around at this place and it still looks the same. Ain't a thing changes," Marcus said as he walked in the car detail shop. You had cars on lifts, and you heard the noise coming from people working on cars around them.

"Come on to the back and tell me what's going on with Frankie. Come in, come in close the door and take a seat."

"As of right now Frankie is in ICU, but he's good. The old man took six shots close range. He's lucky to still be alive."

"That's good he's still alive. Do we know who did it?"

"Not yet, but we are working on it. I'm here to ask a favor from you."

"And what's that?"

"Well, you know about the shipment that was seized so as of right now, I was going to see if I can get a one hundred and fifty flowerpots from you until everything blows over on this little matter."

"Marcus, I would love to, but I received a phone call yesterday from Mr. Russo telling me that Red Invee will be taking control of all Frankie affairs. So, you would have to take that up with Red Invee. I apologize, I can't help you on that matter but if I could you know I would Marcus."

The facial expression Marcus gave when he heard that Red Invee would be taking over all of Frankie's assets was one of death as he bites down on his teeth.

"Mr. Scott, I understand and thank you for your time."

"You're welcome Marcus and give Frankie my love."

"I will," he said as he walked out the door. Once out the detail shop, he called Mr. Russo.

"Hello Mr. Russo, It's Marcus."

"Hello Marcus, how may I help you?"

"I was just told Jamila would be taking over all of the Landon Family assets. Is that true?"

"Yes, it is the request that came from Mr. Landon himself."

"Well, I need to talk with him."

"I'm sorry Marcus. He's in a private hospital right now until he's able to move around again on his own."

"Is there anything I can help with?"

"No, that's it, but if I do need you can I stop by the office?"

"Sure thing anytime, Marcus."

"Ok Mr. Russo. I will contact you if need be. I'll be waiting."

SAYNOMORE

"I'm sorry I was running a little bit behind, but I'm here now."

"It's alright we been talking, and we are willing to let you get the plant at $3.1 million, that's the best we can do."

"Thank you both and we have ourselves a deal."

"So, Lorenzo, does Jamila plan on keeping the same name?"

"No, Jamila plans on changing the name to Sharese Industrial Park."

"Well, it was nice doing business with you as always Lorenzo. And we wish you luck with your new investment."

"Thank you and you two have a bless day. I almost forgot. Jamila is looking for a 7-bedroom house on two acres of land."

"We will keep you in mind and call if anything pops up."

Walking in the conference room you had everyone sitting around waiting on Red Invee to walk in. When she walked in the door all eyes were on her.

"I apologize to everyone I was a little behind. First let me thank all of you for coming. The reason I called this meeting is because we have a unloyal family here today. But who is the question? Red Invee with the upmost respect the Zimmerman family understand why you said that but on the behalf of everyone here. What proof do you have to make the kind of allegation like that?"

"First, Frankie's shipment got tipped off to New Jersey police. Second, they shot Frankie six times in his front yard and Third, they fucked up and tried to kill me. What we do know is that Ms. Simpson shot him. And she tipped off the police on his shipment. The question is who paid her to do it and why. We will find out only when we get her."

"Red Invee, if you don't mind me asking and I'm speaking on the behalf of the Soprano family. It came to me yesterday that you are now running the Landon family for Frankie."

"Yes, I am Mr. Soprano."

"But, why, you and not Marcus?"

"He's been with Frankie for over twelve years and you only been around four years. I think we all would like to know why?"

"Frankie had Marcus contact me and his attorney as well. As Frankie informed me of his wish. From day one I have kept my word with everyone here from drugs to gambling to number running and the night club. I have never tried to move on anyone's turf. But when someone tries to kill me, I take that very personal and to fucking heart. And I'm making this very clear when I find out who it is, I will kill you. With no second thoughts you are dead and who ever tries to stop me they ass is dead too."

"Red Invee let me ask you this. Me and Frankie have been doing a lot of business with each other. Are you going to pick up where we left off at?"

"I'm going over all his financial records now. And to answer your question, yes. I'm just asking that you give me some time to get everything in order, Mr. Saprano."

"I understand that, and I appreciate that Red Invee."

"Red Invee, I have a friend coming from Las Vegas. Do you have any room in one of your 5-star hotels for the Scott family?"

"I do. When will she or he be arriving?"

"This week, Thursday."

"I will have someone call you with the room number. Thank you."

"On behalf of The Genesis, the last time two families went to war we lost over $9 million and I don't want that to happen again. "Is there anything we can do to prevent a war?"

"The LaCross family was attacked and the Landon family was attacked. So, to prevent a war or a bloody massacre again, if someone knows anything, they need to take care of it before it gets out of hand. But we do live by the code of silence. All I'm saying is I help out a lot and all I want is the same respect everyone else gets. Me and my family been through hell and back and we are still standing and we are not falling. Not now or ever. With that being said, I believe we all have an understanding."

"One more thing Red Invee, your actions don't just affect you but all of us."

"Mr. Deniro, you just remember, I ain't throw the first stone somebody else did. With that being said everyone have a nice day," Red Invee said as she walked out.

*****

"Marcus, we need to talk. Where you at?"

"On my way to see Frankie's attorney. What's up?"

"I just got out the meeting of the 7 and Red Invee knows it's someone in the family. But she doesn't know who. The way she's talking it won't be long before she finds out. Clean up all the plate and get rid of all the loose ends."

"And what about Red Invee?"

"I will take care of her myself. Me and Sam is on it."

"Marcus don't fuck this up. I'm warning you."

"I won't," hanging up the phone Marcus walked in Mr. Russo's office.

"Hello, I'm here to see Mr. Russo. Tell him Marcus is here."

"Hold on one moment please. I will let him know you are here."

"Mr. Russo, you have Mr. Marcus here to see you."

"Ok, you can send him back."

Smacking his hands together, "Marcus good afternoon. What can I do for you?"

"Good afternoon Mr. Russo. This won't take up too much of your time. I'm just trying to get an update on Frankie's condition."

"I went to see him yesterday Marcus, he is coming along fine. He should be out of there real soon."

"My question is, why did he want Jamila to take over his assets and not one of us?"

"Marcus, Frankie believes it's someone in the family who had him shot but, who is the question."

"I understand that Mr. Russo. Come take a walk with me just out front. It's a beautiful day plus I don't trust these walls."

"Sure, I can't walk off far, I have a two o'clock that is coming by."

"I promise it won't take long."

As they walked outside down the street, Mr. Russo asked, "Marcus, what is it you wanted to talk to me about?"

"It's on this right here," said Marcus, handing him a folded piece of paper.

Mr. Russo quickly read it. He looked up at Marcus, bewildered. "Marcus, it says *your time is up!* What does that mean?"

Just then Mr. Russo got shot in the back of the head and his body dropped. Marcus kept walking to his car never looking back as Mr. Russo's body just laid on the ground.

SAYNOMORE

Chapter Four

Two Weeks Later...

"Jamila, are you alright?"

"Lorenzo, within the last two weeks Mr. Russo been killed and his assistant both gunned down. We have the FEDS in our backyard now because of this shit with Frankie. And I went to see how his family was doing the other night and things are still running smooth with them. I dropped off 50 kilos so they can still supply they area."

"Well, I got some good news last night. I found out where their keeping Frankie's cocaine at now."

"That's the best news I heard so far."

"Yea, but there's a catch."

"And what's that?"

"For us to get it back, they want $2.5 million, because they have to break in the police building to get it back at the right time."

"Ok set it up for Tuesday at the plant. So how did you find out who had it?"

"I didn't. Marcus called me yesterday and told me he found it.

"How did he know we was looking for it?"

"He told me one of my sources came to him and that's how he found out," replied Lorenzo.

"Tell them to meet us there at 9 p.m. And did you find Ms. Simpson yet?"

"No, but she will be calling soon."

"And why is that?"

"Because we have her son with us now and if she wants to see him again, she knows the rules a life for a life."

"Where are you keeping him at?" asked Jamila.

"Off of Avon in one of Fabio's old houses. It's one acre and its private property so we are good."

"How will she know he's missing?"

"Because it's all over the news already. It's an amber alert. There's something else I want to tell you."

"And what's that?"

"I know who killed Tony Lenacci."

"Who killed him?"

"It was Elisha."

"How do you know this?"

"Before I kidnapped the boy, I was going to have Elisha come with me. And I overheard him talking about it to himself."

"Are you sure?"

"Yea, I am."

"You're telling me Fabio, Isaiah, Abby and Nayana are dead because of him. I've been shot and I killed more muthafuckers than I can count because of him and he never told us."

"You almost died two times and he never said a word."

"You know what Lorenzo, you try and find Ms. Simpson and make all the arrangements to meet up at the plant. And I will take care of Elisha."

"So, what are you about to do now?"

"I'm about to go see an old friend of mine, then I will take care of Elisha."

"Just make sure you do your part."

"Ok, I'll catch up with you in a few."

As Lorenzo walked off his phone went to ringing.

"Hello, it's Marcus."

"What's up Lorenzo? Good timing, I was just waiting to hear from you."

"I'm just now leaving Red Invee. She said we can meet up Tuesday night at the waste plant in Long Island."

"Ok, that works for me. I'll call and let my people know what's up."

"Ok call me back if anything changes Marcus."

"Will do."

Lorenzo hung up the phone and got in his all-black BMW. He turned up the radio playing Jay-Z's the Black Album as he drove off from the docks. As he pulled off, he saw a familiar car riding pass, so he decided to follow it. When the car stopped, he pulled over in the parking lot across the street at a stop and shop. Looking out the window he saw Marcus and Ms. Simpson getting out the car together as they walked in Tony's club, the Red Carpet.

"What the fuck, I know I just ain't see that shit. Now all the pieces are coming together. Marcus set all this shit up. And what do the Lenacci family have to do with any of this."

Waiting for over an hour Lorenzo waited for them to come out. But Marcus never came back out, just Ms. Simpson and she got back in the same blue Ford. Lorenzo waited for it to pull off and he followed it again. Pulling out his phone he called Young Boy.

"Young Boy, where you at? I need you and Badii to meet me at Straight Path. I'm right in front of Pathmark. I'm headed east and hurry up we need to put in some work."

The car pulled up at an old brickhouse. Lorenzo pulled up a few houses down. He watched as Ms. Simpson got out the car. Five minutes later Young Boy and Badii pulled up and got in Lorenzo's car.

"What's up Lorenzo? What needs to be done?"

"Young Boy, look there is one person in that car that I know of. But the one we want is in the house. She's 5'6" white, red hair. Look we need her alive."

"Who else is in the house?"

"I don't know Badii. Me and Young Boy will get him that's in the car. You go check out who is in the house."

"Ya ready? Come on."

Lorenzo walked up to the side of the car. He tapped on the driver's side window. The driver opened the door and put his gun to Lorenzo face, as he got out of the car.

"Who the fuck are you?"

"The landlord of this house."

What he ain't see was Young Boy walking up behind him. Pressing the gun up to the back of his head, "Fuck up and die."

Letting Lorenzo go, he dropped his gun.

"Who else is in the house?" Lorenzo asked, pressing the gun to his head harder.

"My boss asked you a question."

"Nobody just the girl."

Young Boy looked at Lorenzo then smacked the driver in the back of the head, knocking him out cold.

"Get the keys and help get him in the trunk of the car," said Lorenzo.

Badii was looking at Ms. Simpson lying on the couch watching T.V. He saw someone walking back and forth like he was waiting on somebody.

"Badii," Lorenzo said, "I think that's her room over there. Go through the window and wait for her. I'll keep an eye out over here. Young Boy, you go keep an eye out in the front of the house."

Thirty minutes later, Ms. Simpson walked in her bedroom. After her bodyguard checked her room, Badii came from under the bed and put the gun to her head and said, "You yell, you die."

She closed her eyes knowing they found her and there was no way out of it.

"Come on."

"Where are you taking me?"

"Out this window right now."

"Good to see you again, Ms. Simpson."

"Lorenzo, I wish I could say the same thing to you." Ms. Simpson knew she was going to die. The only question was how. Someone wants to see you. When they pulled up at the house Lorenzo opened up the garage door.

"Ms. Simpson follow me please." He walked her to a metal chair, sat her down, and chained her to it. "Badii and Young Boy, I'll see you tomorrow at the plant. Miss Simpson, I don't have no words for you. But I do have one question. Did you really think you was going to get away with it?"

As she lowered her head she said in a low tone, "Where is Red Invee?"

"She will be here in a little while to talk with you," replied Lorenzo as he walked out and closed the door behind him.

Tears was pouring down her face. She knew her actions would catch up with her one day but she ain't think so soon.

*****

Early that morning Lorenzo untied her and let her use the bathroom and he brought her breakfast.

"How am I going to die Lorenzo?"

"What makes you think you are going to die?"

"Lorenzo, please don't give me false hope. I know my hour is at hand."

"Are you done?"

"Yes."

"Can you sit back down so I can tie you back up. Jamila is on her way now."

Opening the door Lorenzo was watching the news when Jamila walked in.

"What's the news talking about?"

"Shit. So how did your meeting go last night?"

"It went well. Are we ready for Tuesday night?"

Sitting down across from Lorenzo he looked at her and said, "Yes, we are all set for Tuesday night."

"Good I can't wait to get this over and done with."

"And I also have something for you Jamila."

"And what is that?"

"Follow me."

When Jamila walked in the garage and saw Ms. Simpson tied to the chair all she could do was smile and shake her head.

"Where did you find her at?"

"With Marcus."

Turning her head looking at Lorenzo, "What the fuck and where's he at?"

"I don't know. I last saw them go in the club. An hour later, she came out. She got in the car and I followed her. Young Boy and Badii helped me get her. I had just gotten off the phone with Marcus and I saw a car I knew from somewhere. I followed it and it pulled up at The Red Carpet and her and Marcus got out. I waited for her to come out and now she's here.

"Do Marcus know we got her?"

"No, nobody does. They were still in the club. She left by herself."

"Ms. Simpson, why the one who took care of you and your family would you try and kill? And tip off the police about his shipment?" asked Jamila.

"The same reason you took on the LaCross family name, because of love."

Jamila knew the feeling to well and how strong love could be. But also, she knew love would get you killed. Looking at Ms. Simpson Jamila grew to love her. She knew her for four years and she knew she had to kill her.

"Well, you should have had more love and loyalty for Frankie because the love you have for Marcus just got you killed. It will be a pain like you never felt before." Then she walked out.

*****

Marcus pulled up at the brick house to see both guards outside and one of them had an ice pack on the back of his head. When he was getting out the car, they walked up to him.

"What the fuck happened now?" ask Marcus.

"She's gone, Marcus."

"What the fuck you mean she gone?"

"I went to check on her like I always do. This morning when I did, she was going out the window. I ran outside to the car and I heard a banging in the trunk of the car and Leo was in the trunk."

"So, what ya telling me is that ya fucked up?"

"And we don't know who got her or where she's at?"

"For your sakes you better hope it's not the LaCross family. I don't know how ya fucked up this up, shit."

"Wait, here I need to make a phone call."

Smoking his cigar Mr. Dinero picked up the phone as he leaned back in his chair.

"Yeah?"

"Mr. Dinero, we have a problem."

"And what's that Marcus?"

"Ms. Simpson is gone, and we don't know where she at."

"What do you mean gone? I don't understand them words because she should be dead."

"The driver was found in the trunk of the car this morning and no one saw her leave."

"So, you are telling me she been kidnapped?"

"Yeah."

"How much do she know?"

"A lot, Mr. Deniro."

"Marcus you know what I don't understand is how you killed everyone who was involved but you let the main one who should have been dead live. After I said clean up all the plates God damn it." Mr. Deniro yelled as he slammed his fist on the desk.

"Now we don't know who got her or what the fuck she said to them."

"This could start a war now because of you."

"I'll take care of it."

"How? How?"

"I don't know yet."

"Marcus, I want you to understand what I'm about to say to you and take this to the heart. Red Invee and Frankie need to be dead and I mean yesterday. I have a meeting with Red Invee Tuesday. I'll have her killed then. I'm still trying to find Frankie."

"You fucked up big Marcus, really big. When you came to me you said you can take care of your part this ain't what I had in mind."

"I have a few strings I ain't pull yet Mr. Deniro. Well, they better play a damn good note with that being said, I'll be in contact Tuesday night when I call, I hope this problem is taken care of."

"Why do you hate Red Invee so much?"

"Let's just say she is in my way and I need her gone."

*****

"Jamila, what now?" Lorenzo asked her as he drunk some water from his glass in the kitchen. We know Marcus is behind all of this and we don't know who else is involved yet.

"Are we still going to have the meeting as planned?"

Yeah, we just know it's a set up that's all. Have Timmy give me a call, I need to talk with him. And we will end this as soon as possible.

"What about Elisha?" asked Lorenzo

"I'm still taking care of that."

"When Frankie getting out the hospital?"

"I don't know yet. I'm going to see him today," said Jamila looking into the woods out the window.

"Lorenzo, I'm going to see Frankie now. This way I can have the rest of the day to handle business. Meet me at Jelani's later."

"Jamila last time you went to see him they tried to kill you up there."

"That's because it was a set up last time. I'll be fine. Make sure everything is set up for tomorrow night. And you make sure you come back to me in one piece." With a laugh in her voice she said, "I will, and I want Ms. Simpson as comfortable as possible Jamila said walking out the door."

*****

The FBI been at the hospital since the day Frankie was brought there, watching who comes in to see him and who they with. Walking in the hospital with her head down Jamila had on a Red hoodie with a black tee shirt under it with some red sweatpants and black Timbs. She had the hood on when she walked in, she ain't notice the FBI agents in the room right across from Frankie's on the private floor. Making her way to Frankie's room she stopped right in her tracks lost for words she was looking at a ghost in the flesh. She was so lost she ain't notice the FBI taking pictures of her. When she opened the door her and Fabio made eye contact. Fabio stood up from the side of Frankie's bed. Tears started falling down Jamila's face at the sight of Fabio. Fabio walked up to Jamila reaching for her hand.

"Jamila let's go somewhere and talk."

"Don't fucking touch me."

"I know what you are thinking right now."

Jamila took two more steps back. "You have no fucking idea what I'm thinking right now. And Frankie knew you was alive all this time?"

"Yes," reaching out to grab Jamila's hand one more time.

She pulled her gun out and pointed it at his head.

"If you try and grab me or take one more towards me, I will push your shit back."

"I know you are upset right now, but you need to calm down. I know you are mad."

"I'm not mad or upset that's an understatement. I'm pissed the fuck off to a whole new level you ain't ready to see. And like I said take one more step towards me and I will pull this trigger."

Looking at Fabio in the face and shaking her head she walked backwards out the room never turning her back on Fabio. Once out the room she ran down the hallway and out the hospital with tears running down her face.

"Jamila," Fabio yelled running behind her before going back in the room with Frankie. Frankie told Fabio how Jamila was doing and making good choices but out of all the things he told him he never told him how good she looked or smelled. Just seeing her after two years made him weak for her again. He needed to get her to sit down and talk with him just for a moment. Returning to Frankie's bedside Fabio said, "I'm here and I'm not going nowhere ever again. I'm back now for good." He then walked out the room the way he came in. All he could do was think about Jamila and how he can get her to trust him again.

Once Jamila made it back to her car she started screaming and punching the steering wheel as flashbacks of the shooting in Jelani's went through her head. Looking at Fabio as Frankie rushed him to the back, and just to hear the words Frankie said to her four years ago ripped a hole in her heart. Fabio's body gave up on him, making her scream even louder, as she put the car in gear and drove off.

SAYNOMORE

Chapter Five

"Detective Boatman, why do you think Jamila LaCross came to visit a crime boss?"

"That's a good question."

"Because that's not good for her image."

"Why do you think Agent Smith?"

"I think there's more to her than we know about. So, we need to pull up everything we know about her and Frankie somehow."

"I'm on it, Agent Smith."

"And who is this guy with the baseball cap on?"

"I don't know. I couldn't see his face he had a hoodie and baseball cap on."

"But his name on Frankie's visitation says Brian Oldham."

"Boatman run his name too, when you get back to the station."

"I'll get on it as soon as I walk through the doors."

*****

Jamila wouldn't say a word to anyone when she made it back to the restaurant. She ignored everyone as she made her way to her office. She slammed the door closed to get her thoughts together. The man she loved; the one she trusted, had her believing he was a liar, and that changed her heart. She looked at the picture taken of her and Fabio the first time he took her to Paris with him. More tears ran down her face as she made her way to the mini bar. She opened a bottle of gray goose and took four shots back-to-back. She reminisced about the pictures that was sent to her of Isaiah's kidnaping and killing. And how the man she loved betrayed her.

Jamila made her mind up Fabio was dead in her eyes with Nayana and Isaiah. And if he tries to meet up with her, she will kill him her fucking self.

When Lorenzo opened the door and saw the look on Jamila's face, he knew something was wrong. But he didn't ask her; he knew when she was ready to talk, she would. Taking one more shot looking at Lorenzo, from here on out we play by our own rules and for keeps. If we break the rules who gives a fuck. We are our own fucking law breakers.

"Jamila is there something you want to talk to me about?"

"No is everything ready for tomorrow night?"

"Yea, so what are we going to do, we know it's a set up?"

"I know, I got this. Is Ms. Simpson still at the house?"

"Yea she is Badii with her."

"I'll go talk to her you stay here and close up. And I'll see you tomorrow night before the meeting."

"Ok, I got this, and I'll see you then."

*****

Walking in the house Jamila wasn't in her right state of mind. Miss Simpson was still tied up to the chair.

"Badii did you feed her and give her something to drink?"

"Yea I did a few hours ago."

"Ok, go back in the room with little man until I call you."

Leaning against the garage door, Jamila looked at her as she slept in the chair thinking she should put her gun to her fucking head and blow her brains out and stepping in the garage as her heels hit the floor.

"Wake up we need to talk."

"About what, how you going to kill me?"

"I'm not going to kill you, but you will tell me what I need to know."

Looking up at Jamila, "And what you need to know?"

"Who is helping Marcus out?"

"I don't know what you mean."

Jamila walked up to the garage door and picked up the shovel and smacked Ms. Simpson so hard in her face that the chair flipped backwards. She then smacked her in the face again with the shovel as she laid on the garage floor.

Looking down at her she said, "now I'll ask you one more fucking time and think about what the fuck you say."

Picking her up off the floor she had blood coming from her lip and a cut under her eye.

"Before you answer that question just know I have your son. So, think about what I just asked you."

"Please Jamila," said Ms. Simpson, "don't hurt my son."

"I won't if you tell me what I want to know." Crossing her arms looking at her, "I'm waiting."

In a low tone looking up at Jamila, "it's the Deniro family. They are helping Marcus. Marcus wanted Frankie's family and the deal was to knock you off. And the Deniro family would be moving into Queens but first they had to get Frankie out the way. They knew Frankie has been helping you since the war with the Lenacci family."

"So why were you at the Red Carpet?"

"Because Marcus was trying to get the Lenacci family to help them with you. But they wanted no part of it. Before I left Vinnie told Marcus if they try you, they will be signing they own death certificate."

"So, what else?"

"Marcus set up the hospital shooting, and he had me make the call to the police about Frankie shipment and give me the gun to kill him that morning."

"Where is Marcus at now?"

"At one of the Deniro family houses in Long Island I told you they are helping him. That all I know I swear. What about my son now?"

"I'll let you talk with him in a few minutes." Jamila untied Ms. Simpson and cleaned her up and walked her to the backroom.

"Where Badii and her son were watching cartoons."

"Mommy, Mommy," he said, jumping in her arms.

Jamila waved for Badii to come on.

"I'll be back in a little while Ms. Simpson."

*****

Walking in the backyard Marcus saw Mr. Deniro eating at his picnic table with a few men around him.

"Mr. Deniro, we have everything in place for tomorrow night when she come to make the deal as soon as she gets out the car she will be killed. I have a guy on the roof waiting for her to step out of the car."

"And how do you know it's going to be her and not Lorenzo?"

"Because Red Invee likes to be a part of everything and this is for Frankie, so it's personal for her."

"Let's get this over with as soon as possible. It's set up for tomorrow night at 9 p.m."

"Call me when it's done."

"I will, sir."

As Marcus was walking off, Deniro called him.

"Marcus?"

"Yea?"

"If you fuck this up just know you will pay with your life."

Marcus looked at him and walked off.

Walking in the room Ms. Simpson was rubbing her son's back as he was sleeping. "I kept my word, now I'll give you a chance to stay in your son's life."

"What I need to do?"

"Tomorrow night you are going to deliver a message to Marcus for me. He thinks I'm meeting him. But you are. I'll let you talk to him face to face. You are going to drive my car and I'll be watching just in case you try me."

"I won't I swear."

"I got something for you, I'll be right back."

Walking out the room Jamila came back a few minutes later with a plate of food and a bag in her hands. "Here's something to eat. Don't worry, it's not poison."

"Jamila, I know if you wanted me dead, I would be dead already."

"Tomorrow night when you see Marcus, let him know he fucked up. And give him this suitcase for me. Jamila opened it up to show her it's not a bomb inside. See it's just a piece of paper."

She closed the suitcase and opened the window and placed the bag of clothes on the bed.

"I hope I got your size right."

"What about my son?"

"He will be dropped off at your mother's tomorrow night. You have my word. He's been with me for one week now and no harm came to him yet, right? You know I could be very cold hearted. So, I'm leaving you and him here and I'm not tying you up. But don't fuck with me because if you try and run when I do catch you, I'll feed him to my dogs and make you watch, That I promise. You have a nice night Ms. Simpson."

Walking out the room Jamila knew Ms. Simpson couldn't let nothing happened to her son, so she wasn't worried about her leaving. Still lightheaded from the shots she had earlier. She had so much hate in her heart for Fabio she could kill him, but a part of her heart still loved him unconditionally.

*****

"Jamila you need to clear your head and be focused tonight," said Lorenzo to her as she was looking in her birdcage.

"I'm focused, I just got a lot on my mind." Walking away from her birdcage and going to the table grabbing an apple out of the basket. Looking at Lorenzo as his phone went off.

"Hello, it's Marcus. Is everything ready for tonight?"

"Yeah, I talked to Red Invee. She's going to meet you there and I'll catch up to you two later on in the night. I have something else I need to deal with."

"Ok, I'll see you later on tonight then."

"Facts, I'll see you then."

"Mr. Marcus Landon, I take it?"

"Yea, Jamila are you sure this is going to work?"

"Yea, I'm sure don't worry trust me."

"Marcus is ready and I'll see you in a few."

Wait, before you go, I have something to tell you.

"What's that?"

"After all of this is done, I'm cutting all ties with Frankie and his family."

"Why is that?"

"He's been lying to us and when I went to see him guess who was there."

"Who?"

"Fabio."

"Jamila, Fabio is dead."

"No, Lorenzo, Fabio is not dead. He is very much alive, but we will talk about this later. We have to keep focus tonight. So, let me run and get Ms. Simpson now."

Ms. Simpson was dressed and ready to go, when Jamila pulled up to meet Marcus at the waste plant.

"You look beautiful!"

"Jamila what you think he's going to say to me?"

"I don't know let me walk you to the car. Remember I will be watching you."

"I know you will be."

Backing out the yard Ms. Simpson was driving Jamila's car to the Waste plant. Jamila called Lorenzo.

"Hey, she's on her way now," said Jamila.

"I'm waiting on you."

"I'll be there in twenty minutes. I'm taking the back roads."

Lorenzo was watching everything from the second floor of the building. He saw when Marcus pulled up and backed the truck up in the parking lot. Jamila walked up through the back door.

"Is she here yet?"

"She's pulling up now."

Jamila watched as she pulled up and parked the car. Stepped out with the briefcase in her hand. Marcus was standing in front of his truck with the high beams on. Before she could take a step forward her body hit the ground from a sniper fifty yards away. Marcus ran to get the suitcase and was in shock to see Ms. Simpson laying there dead instead of Red Invee. He picked up the suitcase and ran back to the truck and him and Deniro's man drove off. When he opened up the suitcase, he saw there was a note inside.

"What they say Marcus?"

Picking up his phone, "Hello?"

"Marcus you fucked up and Deniro fucked up. It's a shame you killed Ms. Simpson but I'll tell you this. My bullets won't hit the wrong person. Sleep on that."

"She fucking knows, shit, shit. Call Mr. Deniro and tell him what happened."

"I'm telling you now Marcus he's not going to be pleased about this at all."

Pulling out his phone he called.

"Boss, it's Johnny."

"How it goes?"

"She knew it was a set up and the wrong target was hit."

"Where's Marcus at?"

"Right here boss."

"Can he hear me?"

"No, Sir."

"Kill him."

"Marcus, the boss wants to speak to you. Here's the phone."

"Hello"

Boom.

"Damn Johnny you could of gave me a heads up. Mr. Deniro said kill him, so I pushed his brains out the window. Now open the door and push his body out and let's go burn this truck."

Picking up the phone. "Hello boss, you still there?"

"Yeah."

"It's done boss."

"I heard now come to the house."

"We on our way."

*****

"Jamila you saw that? They were setting you up from the jump to kill you."

"I was ready for it that's why I had Ms. Simpson go in my place."

"What are we going to do now?"

"Call and have her body picked up and taken to the morgue. Even though she tried to kill Frankie I understand her feelings. Look at how many people I killed over Fabio."

"Come on let's go down there and look at her, she ain't even know she was going to die today."

"She did Lorenzo. I overheard her tell her son, mommy going to be an angel watching over you real soon. Call Badii and have him take her son to his grandmother's house tonight and I'll meet you inside the waste plant."

*****

"Mr. Deniro, she knew it was a set up. She wasn't even driving the car. She had Ms. Simpson driving and as soon as she stepped out the car, she was shot dead."

Sitting behind his desk eating a sandwich Mr. Deniro said, "The nigga is smart."

"So, what we going to do now Boss?"

Johnny was still wiping Marcus's blood off his hands with a rag.

"We're going to play everything by ear. We don't know what Ms. Simpson told her."

"You sure you just don't want to take Red Invee down and get it over with?"

"That cat is out the bag now."

Deniro put his sandwich down on the desk and wiped his mouth off. "Johnny, look at what happened to the Lenacci family behind her. If we do, we have to make our first move and make it count. But as of right now, just make sure they ready for anything at any time."

"I'll go take care of that now."

"Johnny you know I put my trust in you."

"I know boss."

Chapter Six

The Next Day…

"Mrs. LaCross you have a phone call on line one."

"Ok, I'll take it in my office." As Jamila walked in her office she sat down and picked up the phone.

"Ms. LaCross speaking hello."

"Jamila, please don't hang up the phone. Can you hear what I got to say? Just hear me out for one second."

"For what? I've never spoken to a dead person before."

"I have my reason why I did what I did. Can we just meet somewhere and talk?"

"Fabio, I'm not going to say what's on my mind because this is my place of business. But I will meet you this one time and only this one time. Meet me by Central Park by the water fountain and you only have five minutes."

"I respect that. What time Jamila?"

"Tomorrow at 1 p.m. and remember you only have five minutes after that," she hung the phone up. Fabio looked at his phone and placed it down next to him on the couch. Watching the news, he saw Marcus's body being found. His name ran across the front of the TV screen. He knew there was more to his death. He was shot close range one time in the head.

"Damn Marcus. What did you do?"

Getting up wondering how he was going to tell Jamila he was very sorry for leaving her. The last thing he remember was laying on the bed looking up at her when Frankie took him to the back, she said I love you baby as she was holding his hand. Now seeing her face to face is going to be hard. The only question he wants to know is can she trust him or love him again. For the last four years Fabio stayed in contact with Frankie. Frankie told him how Jamila took over the southside of Queens with a bloody fight. Bodies were found everywhere. Car bombs were going off.

NYC Post called it the worst year in the city's history. Jamila did what no one else could. She killed Tony Lenacci. Then his heads she proved she was a boss bitch and not to be fucked with. All the families respected her. And he lost her because he left her when she needed him the most. Frankie said her name held respect and he also told him about the politicians she had in her pocket. Jamila had a Fortune 500 mind, and she was using it. Over the years she had up to 40 plus people killed. It was hard for a lot of people to take a black female as a Don.

Now the only women who saved his life and killed over him who he betrayed is going to meet up with him. Tomorrow but this ain't the same lady he once knew. This is Red Invee the female Don over the LaCross family.

*****

"Mrs. Jackson, we need the rooms upstairs cleaned."

"Can you have housekeeping take care of that for us?" Elisha was now running one of Jamila's 5-star hotels in Queens named Destiny. He was on the phone when Jamila walked in. "Hold on Mrs. Jackson, can you take this call please?"

"Sure."

"Hello Ms. Jackson."

"Good afternoon Ms. LaCross."

"Elisha let's go somewhere and talk."

"We can go to the ballroom nobody is in there. It's booked for tomorrow night."

Jamila followed Elisha in the ballroom and sat down at the table. The look in her eyes, Elisha knew something was wrong.

"So, tell me Elisha, how are things going here?"

"Jamila, you could have called if you wanted to know that. What's the real reason you are here?"

"If you want me to get to the point, I will. I want to know why Elisha, why did you do it? And ain't let nobody know."

Elisha looked down at the floor. "How did you find out?"

"It's not important how I found out. Isaiah's dead. Nayana's dead. Abby and your whole family are dead too. You put us in harm's way. I've been shot. Lorenzo was fighting for his life. For what? Why did you do it? How can you say you love us and never told us?"

"Jamila every day I have to look in the mirror and face myself. I hate myself for what I did. I don't know why I did it. I'm sorry for the ones I hurt and the ones we lost. Tears started falling down Elisha's face as he told Jamila he was sorry. I wanted to tell you so many times, I did. I was scared too. I don't know why. When I cut his throat I just wanted to see if I can get away with it. I ain't know everything that would come behind my actions."

"Elisha you killed the boss of all bosses. Tony Lenacci. What you think would happened?"

Elisha got up and hugged Jamila. "I love you!" Jamila knew in her heart there was no turning back. Tears were in her the eyes.

Jamila whispered in his ear as she hugged him, "I love you more!"

Elisha knew in his heart he was about to die. "Jamila, how are you going to do this?"

"Turn around."

Elisha closed his eyes and turned around and dropped to his knees. Jamila pulled a .38 out of her purse with a silencer on it and pointed it at his head. Right before she pulled the trigger she said, "sleep in peace. I love you Elisha."

With one pull of the trigger his body hit the floor. Jamila got on her hands and knees and turned his body over. Kissing his cheek tears started falling down her face. She stood up and walked to the bar and took a shot for him. She then dragged his body behind the bar. She walked out the ballroom and locked the door behind her placing a DO NOT ENTER sign on the door. When Elisha ain't come back out the ballroom, Ms. Jackson knew what happened. She been working for Ms. LaCross for three years. She knew that she would be taking his place. Jamila called Lorenzo.

"I need you to clean up a mess at Destiny's. It is in the ballroom behind the bar."

Lorenzo knew exactly what she was talking about. "Ok, I'm on my way."

"Thank you."

"Ms. Jackson."

"Yes, Ms. LaCross?"

"You are now the manager of this hotel. I'll see you sometime this week to go over the paperwork with you, said Jamila as she walked out."

*****

Fabio was at the park waiting for Jamila to show up. He kept looking at his watch. Everyone walked pass him from the kids playing catch to the old lady walking the dog. He stood up to see if he could see her. It was 1:25 pm, Jamila was watching Fabio from the bridge the whole time. In her mind he made her wait four years, he could wait twenty-five minutes. She started to walk down the bridge to meet Fabio. She was wearing a thin pair of gray sweatpants and matching gray hoodie. She had the gray and white bunny rabbit Jordan's on with a pair of black shades covering her face. Her hair was curled down coming out of her hoodie. When Fabio saw her, he walked up to her to give her a hug. Jamila stopped him.

"I ain't come here for that. What you want to talk about?"

"Can we at least sit down and talk?" replied Fabio. When they sat down Fabio said, "I am truly sorry for all that I put you through."

"Please Fabio," said Jamila, "save me the apology speech I'm over it, trust me." Jamila still loved Fabio. She just ain't want to show it.

"Jamila, can you please just let me say what I have to say."

"Just remember you have five minutes then I'm leaving."

"I respect that." Looking at her he was lost for words.

"Jamila, I can't take back what I done. I thought if they thought I was dead they would leave you alone. I wanted to reach out to you so many times it was killing me to know you was out here without me. Frankie told me everything you was doing and kept me up to date all the time. I'm just asking, can we take this one step at a time and try this again between the two of us? You and Frankie are all I have in this world."

Jamila got up and looked at him. "Did I just hear you right? Did you just hear what the fuck you said? Frankie kept you up to date when Jelani's burnt down, you were up to date. The shoot outs you were up to date. My friends being killed you was up to date. And you going to come to me with this weak ass sorry. Nigga, I killed my best friend because she was trying to set you up. All this time I thought you was dead and you're telling me you were up to date. Fuck boy, stay the fuck out my face and I'm telling you this now, so you are up to date." Jamila felt tears about to come down her face. She hated Fabio at that point in time, but she knew he still loved her, and he was sorry for his action. But that meant nothing to her. She looked at Fabio and said, "We are done."

Looking at her, "Jamila wait. I know you are upset."

"Bye Fabio," she said as she walked off.

Fabio watched Jamila as she walked away. As much as he wanted to, he ain't say another word. He just watched her until he couldn't see her no more.

Jamila was so upset that she came to see Fabio. His words touched her like never before. She never felt like this before about a man.

Getting in her car as she went to pull off out the parking lot, four FBI trucks cut her off.

"Fuck, this is all I need. What the fuck they want?" When they got out the truck's detective Boatman and a female agent walked up to Jamila's car.

"Ms. LaCross, can you step out the car?"

"May I ask you why? And who are you?"

"I'm FBI agent Walker and this is NYPD Detective Boatman."

Jamila looked at the young white agent with her black suit on and red hair, as she got out the car.

Detective Boatman walked up to her. He was 5'9" bald- head black, brown eyes with a beard.

"Can you follow me Ms. LaCross to this truck?"

"Am I under arrest?"

"No, but we need to ask you some questions."

"Well detective, I have an attorney. You can ask all the questions you want too."

"That's good to know. You can call him when we get to the station."

Jamila sat in the truck next to the agent. Walking in the investigation room, "Ms. LaCross have a seat. My name is Agent Watts. I bring you here to ask you, how do you know Frankie Landon?"

"Agent Watts it is right?"

"Yes."

"Ok, just like I told your field officers, I have an attorney to answer all your questions and I would like to call him now if you do not mind. Other than that, I don't have nothing to say."

"Ok, Ms. LaCross." The agent walked out the room.

"What you think Walker?"

"She's tough. She's not going to say nothing. She is following the code of silence. We had her for over an hour. Well Watts, we did what we needed to do. We bugged her car."

"Ok Walker let her go then."

"Ms. LaCross you can leave. If you don't mind following me and here are your car keys."

Jamila knew well enough that they bugged her car. So, she didn't pick up her phone or play the radio. She dropped her car off at the bus station and took a cab to the restaurant. She told Lorenzo what happened with her and where her car was at.

"So, what happened with Fabio?"

"He told me why he faked his death and how sorry he was."

"So, what you say to him?"

"Nothing. After he said what he said I walked off and never looked back. Did you clean that mess up at Destiny's?"

"Yea, I did. Did it hurt you to do that?"

"Whether it hurt me or not, it had to be done. One thing I will not accept in this family is disloyalty."

"So where do we go from here?"

"Lorenzo, I need some time to myself. I'm going to Miami for a few weeks. Do you think you can run things while I'm gone?"

"Yea, I got this. What about the Deniro family?"

"We are going to keep them in the dark until I know more than we are going to deal with them."

"So, when you plan on leaving?"

"Tonight, I'll see you when I get back."

*****

Walking in the police station Detective Boatman went to his office and sat down behind his desk and turned his computer on. Pulling up files on all the Mafia families in NYC that's when his phone went off. "Detective Boatman, it's Chief Tadem, come to my office."

"I'm on my way sir."

Opening his bottom desk draw he pulled out a folder and walked out his office. He saw a few faces he never seen before as he made it to the Cheif's office, knocking on the door.

"Come in detective have a seat. How are you doing today?"

"Good sir."

"I called you in here so you can tell me what you have on Jamila."

"She's clean. We been watching her for the past few weeks, after her name came up after Frankie's shooting. All of her establishments are legit. From the time she wakes up she drives to Central Park and runs for an hour. She has these two guys always watching her. They are her bodyguards." Detective Boatman handed Chief Tadem two pictures. "The tall one name is Derrick Park A.K.A. Young Boy and the other one name is Anthony Wright A.K.A Badii. After her run, she goes to Starbucks and gets a cup of coffee. She makes it back home by 11:45 am."

"What time do she leave her house?"

"Every day at 8:30am sir. She leaves her house by 1 pm and stops by all her establishments starting with Destiny's, the hotel. She sees her manager there his name is Elisha. Here's a picture of him."

"Where do I know that name from?"

"Well four years ago Cheif, his whole family was killed, and the house set on fire. He was shot 8 times and was found two blocks over laying in the road."

"You know what Boatman I remember that case. Okay, go on."

"After she leaves Destiny's she stops by a night club called *Passions* and here's a picture of Kent who runs the place for her. When she leaves there, she heads to Jelani's and stays there for the rest of the day. Now outside of that every Thursday she goes to the cemetery to pay her respects to her friends. She always puts white and red roses down. And she always goes there alone."

"Is there a man in her life?"

"No, not that we know of."

"What about the guy in the park?"

"You ready for this, we found out who he was. At first, we didn't know when we saw him at the hospital. The man we saw at the hospital and the park is Fabio LaCross."

"Wait, I thought he got killed a few years back."

"We all did. It turns out he faked his death. We can pick him up on that, that's against the law."

"Not exactly, I went deeper into that. Fabio's parents were killed by the Lenacci family. So, they were after him too. So, with that being said his attorney talked to the mayor and it was approved."

"Ok now back to Jamila. Where did she get all this money from?"

"After Fabio faked his death, he left her $4 million plus Jelani's and she just made some smart investments."

"So, we can't get her on anything?"

"Not even a parking ticket. So, let me finish. She got a new business in Long Island. It's a Waste plant called Sharese Industry. Last week we had a P.I follow her down there. Now the P. I. thought it was her he was following down there. When the lady got out the car, she was shot dead to the head and two more times afterwards we have pictures. Now Marcus was there too. You do remember Marcus's body was found on the side of the road last week."

"Ok, I remember that."

"He was there that night. He ran and picked up a briefcase out of her hands. The lady who was killed now wait till I tell you who she was. Ms. Simpson, Frankie's maid for seven years and moments later Marcus was killed."

"So how are all these dots being put together Boatman?"

"Ok, Cheif, first Jersey police got a tip on a big shipment of cocaine. Then the man who shipment it was gets shot six times the same day. After that there's a big shoot out at the hospital who we think the mystery Detective is Jamila. Because whoever she was they tried to kill her. Now when Fabio came back from the dead in all this mix Ms. Simpson and Marcus get killed at one of Jamila's new establishments not to mention Frankie's lawyer and friend gets killed 3 blocks away from his office and his assistant and who ever killed Ms. Simpson. Who I think they really was after Jamila?"

"Let's pick Jamila up for the body at the waste dump."

"We can't because she was never there."

"What about this Lorenzo?"

"Hell, we think he's her second in command, but we don't know yet. All we know about him is that he's always at Jelani's. When he leaves there, he goes home. I really haven't been focused on him too much."

"Well put a team on him he might be our weak link."

"One more thing, Cheif. Do you remember four years ago the big Mob War?"

"Yeah, a lot of big hittas got killed."

"Well, what we do know is the LaCross family was responsible for it and Jamila is the head of the LaCross family. And you know the Lenacci family use to run part of south side Queens. Now the LaCross family runs all of it. I just thought you might want to know that."

"I see she's more than a pretty face, more like Bloody Mary herself."

"No, Cheif, she's the new Tony Lenacci. I'll put a team on Lorenzo and let's see what we come up with. You never know he might be our fish we catch on the hook."

SAYNOMORE

Jamila knew the FBI was watching her. Mr. Russo told her they were asking questions about the Detective who went to see Frankie that night. She wasn't trying to take any chances in her movements, she knew the FEDS was following her. She just hoped Lorenzo ain't mess up. She got word to Morwell about what was going on and how she needed to watch the way she moved. She also had a conversation with Vinnie and told him she needed to stop wasting money for a short period of time. Because she is being watched by the FEDS and she don't want nothing to come back on the Lenacci family because of her. Jatavious told her they were fishing and they had nothing on her. He read over her file already as of right now she's clean. As much as she didn't want to go, she needs some time to get herself together after everything that was going on.

Chapter Seven

It was stormy outside you heard the roar of the thunder and the lightning flashed across the skies, the rain as Fabio looked out of the hospital window. Frankie woke up out of his coma. When he saw Fabio, he said in a very weak voice, "Fabio."

"Frankie don't talk. Let me go get a nurse."

"May I help you?"

"Yes, I just came out of room 211. Mr. Frankie Landon just woke up out of his coma."

As they walked back in the room the nurse checked all his signs.

"Everything looks good let me go get the doctor he will be here in a few. "

"Frankie, I been worried sick about you."

"Fabio you came back."

"When I heard what happened, I been here ever since."

Just then the doctor walked in the room. "Mr. Frankie Landon, good to see you up. How long have you been up?"

"Maybe five minutes the most," said Fabio.

"Well, the good news is all your vital signs are good."

"How long have I been in a coma?"

"Four months."

"Well Mr. Landon everything looks good. You made a full recovery, but I do want to run some more test tomorrow when you are better rested." The doctor left the room.

"Fabio where's Jamila?"

"I don't know she been up here a few times to check on you."

"Why did you come back?"

"I couldn't leave you like this you needed me so here I am."

"Did Jamila see you?"

"Yea that's a long story we will talk about on another day."

"Where is Marcus at?"

"Dead and so is Mr. Russo and Ms. Simpson."

"Call Jamila, I need to talk to her."

"Frankie relax, you just woke up after four months in a coma. We will reach out to her tomorrow." Frankie closed his eyes knowing a lot has gone on.

Fabio walked out the room to call Jamila, but it went right to voicemail. He tried a few more times before going back in the room with Frankie.

"Frankie, I have to make a run, I'll be back in a few hours."

"I'll be here."

Fabio went to Jelani's thinking Jamila might be there. When he walked in all eyes was on him. Everyone who he had working there was still there. Jamila got rid of no one. He turned around to see Lorenzo looking at him.

Making his way to Fabio.

"Good to see you Fabio."

"You too, Lorenzo."

"Is there some place we can talk?"

"Follow me."

They made their way to Lorenzo's office.

"Please have a seat."

"Funny, I don't remember this office being here."

"That's because we just had it put here when the restaurant burnt down."

"How have you been Lorenzo?"

"Good. Jamila told me you were alive. Now here I am looking face to face at you."

"Where is Jamila?" Fabio asked.

"She is gone. She will be back in a few weeks."

"Do you have a way to contact her? She cut off her phone."

"No," replied Lorenzo, "Why what's up?"

"Frankie wants to see her. He is out of his coma."

"That's good. I have an address waiting on him. Let's get him out that hospital."

"What do you mean you have an address waiting on him?"

"Jamila went and got him a private house where nobody knows but me and her for his recovery."

Fabio kept looking around his office and stopped when he saw a picture of Jamila and Jatavious Stone on the wall.

"Where is this house at?"

"I'll take you and Frankie there tomorrow."

"Why can't you tell me where the house is at and I'll bring Frankie there?"

"Because Jamila told me what she wants done and I'm following her orders."

"Her orders?"

Lorenzo loosened up his tie. "Fabio for the last four years Jamila has taken care of everything. Fabio when you left, or should I say faked your death in four years she turned $4 million into $20 million. She has ties in stocks and bonds up to $30 million or more give or take. I respect your bond with Frankie, but she also has a very strong bond with him too. Out of respect for Frankie you and Jamila need to see eye to eye for him. I will take you to the house tomorrow morning."

Fabio knew Lorenzo was right, so he agreed. "So, what time tomorrow would you like to meet up?"

"Be ready by 5 am."

"Why so early?"

"So, we will know if we are being followed. I'll see you then."

Fabio shook Lorenzo's hand and walked out of Jelani's knowing he made the right choice with Jamila. He just hopes she could forgive him for what he done.

Lorenzo watched as Fabio walked out the door then he walked back in his office and closed the door.

*****

Lorenzo pulled up at the hospital 4:30 that morning. When Frankie came outside, he had two bodyguards with him and Fabio. They helped Frankie downstairs to the limo.

"Frankie it's good to see you up and running again."

"It's good to be up too, Lorenzo," giving him a kiss and a hug.

"Lorenzo tells me what I been missing for the last four months."

"Frankie if you don't mind can you and I have a conversation when we get to the house. We should be there in thirty-five to forty-five minutes."

Frankie nodded his head and looked out the window. He had so many questions he needed answers to. So, he just sat back and made a mental note of all that he could remember before the shooting.

When they pulled up to the house Fabio was shocked that Jamila had done all of this for Frankie. The house had ten men walking around on the grounds with two canines and fifteen cameras when they made it inside the den. Lorenzo went and got Mr. Lawrence the head of security.

"Mr. Lawrence this is Frankie Landon your new boss from here on out."

"Nice to meet you Mr. Landon."

"Likewise."

"Mr. Landon if you need me, I'll be walking the grounds. Here is a radio we all have one you can call me on this if you need me."

"Thank you, I will."

"Lorenzo what is all of this?"

"Red Invee said as long as she lives nothing will ever happen again. So, let me catch you up on things."

"Please do so."

"After Jamila came to see you at the hospital that night someone tried to kill her in the parking lot. There was a big shoot out. The next day she went and saw Mr. Russo, three days later he was killed and his assistant. Now out the blue Marcus called me and said he knew where your drugs was being held and to get them back it will cost $2.5 million so Red Invee said set it up."

"Wait hold up Lorenzo, who is Red Invee?"

"Fabio, that's Jamila's underground name."

"Ok."

"So, we set it up but in the mix of all of this I saw a car that looked familiar, so I followed it. When the car stopped Marcus and Ms. Simpson got out together."

"Hold on, Lorenzo you are telling me Marcus and Ms. Simpson were behind all of this?"

"Yea he was after we kidnapped Ms. Simpson, she told us everything from Marcus having her call the police about your shipment to having her shoot you. Marcus was trying to take over your family that's why he killed Mr. Russo and the Deniro family was helping him. They tried to get help from the Lenacci family, but they wanted no parts in it."

"So how Ms. Simpson get killed?"

"Red Invee set it up and Marcus killed her without even knowing it was her. We don't know who killed Marcus. But we know there is a private investigator watching us. We saw them following Ms. Simpson the night she was killed."

"So where is Red Invee now?"

"When Fabio came back it was a lot on her, so she left for a few weeks to clear her mind up."

"So, the Deniro family and the man I trusted tried to kill me?"

"Yea they did and Red Invee told me not to do anything until she gets back."

"Lorenzo, Frankie is back now I think he can handle things from here on out."

"With all due respect Fabio, I think Frankie can speak for himself. With that being said when Red Invee gets back in town I will have her reach out to you. Until then Frankie here is a number you can reach out to me on."

Lorenzo handed Frankie a piece of papers with his number on it.

"Thank you, Lorenzo."

"No problem Frankie."

When Lorenzo turned around to walk out the room Fabio called out to him, when he turned around Fabio and Lorenzo were face to face.

"Lorenzo, I don't know what the deal is with you. Just remember I gave you and Jamila all of this and don't forget it. I'm back now and respect my mind frame."

Lorenzo looked at Fabio like he was crazy.

"Fabio, I want you to hear me and hear me very fucking well. You might have given Red Invee all of this but it came with a fucking price. Two of our friends are dead behind you. She's been shot two times. My friend's family is dead. Every day Red Invee must look over her shoulder. While you were sleeping somewhere very fucking peacefully. We were here having shoot outs, kidnappings and murders so you just remember that. And if she does let you back in her life again and you hurt her again. I will kill you my fucking self and burn your fucking body. Now Fabio take that to the fucking heart. Jump motherfucker, try me." Lorenzo looked at him and walked off. When Lorenzo went back to the limo he pages Red Invee 2040 that meant call as soon as possible.

Chapter Eight

"Mr. Deniro, where are we going from here?"

"We don't know what Marcus told Ms. Simpson and we don't know what Ms. Simpson told Red Invee."

"Johnny, Red Invee knew it was a set up."

"Why do you think she had Ms. Simpson driving her car?"

"And I'm willing to bet she was somewhere the whole time watching."

Deniro picked up the pool stick and hit the stripped ball in the hole. As Johnny talked to him in the pole hall. With his cigar in his mouth biting down on it he looked up right before he was about to take another shot.

"Johnny if we start a war with her, we will end up just like the Lenacci family."

Putting his pool stick down and standing straight up.

"Johnny, Red Invee has too many politicians, judges and DA's in her pockets. We have to catch her slipping. When Red Invee ask us and she will, I will say we are at war with the Landon family not you. And I am sorry for whatever Marcus had you thinking. And when I found out about his actions, I had him killed. Then Johnny the first chance we get 8 ball corners pockets, the nigga is dead. Now if you don't mind, I'd like to get back to my game."

"Mr. Deniro, so we are at war with the Landon family."

"We are now. Frankie is weak he has been slipping for a while now."

"So, do you want me to start moving on his turf?"

"Not yet but he does have a warehouse in New Jersey right off of Avon. That's where he makes and bakes all of his cocaine and heroin. Let's set something up and let's put a burner in his pocket."

"I'm on it now."

"Good."

*****

Jamila heard a knock at the door, she throws the covers over her head then got up. When she opened the door, it was room service bringing her a breakfast tray. She forgot she order last night for one to be brought to her in the morning. Walking back to her bed she placed the tray on the bed and looked to see Lorenzo paged her yesterday 2040. She picked up the phone after it ranged twice.

"Hey what's up Lorenzo?"

"Frankie is out the hospital. I brought him to the new house. He also asked about you."

"I told you when he wakes up, we are done with him and his family."

"That's all I needed to hear and me and Fabio had words."

"About what?"

"Basically, he said we need to remember he gave us all that we have and don't forget it."

"Are you serious?"

"Dead ass. I blew on him and told him it came at a fucking price."

"I don't believe him you know what let him handle all Frankie's' business now. I'll be back in three days."

"How is everything on our end?" Jamila asked.

"Good no worries."

"That's what I like to hear. I'll see you when you get back."

"I'll be waiting. Enjoy the rest of your vacation."

"Thanks."

Jamila laid the phone down and said to herself. "Fuck Fabio. He keeps fucking with me he's going to be on someone's t-shirt talking to his mother and father."

After hanging up the phone Lorenzo walked inside Jelani's there, he found Mr. Deniro, Gino and his men waiting for him. They all were sitting down at the table waiting for him.

Lorenzo walked to the table and Mr. Deniro got up to greet him. They shook hands. Mr. Deniro had a smile on his face.

"Lorenzo, good morning!"

"Is it a good morning Mr. Deniro?"

"I'm hoping it is. Can we go somewhere and talk?"

"Sure, my office is this way, please follow me. Just you and Gino. Your men can order whatever breakfast they want. It's on the house."

"Ya heard him order what ya like I'll be back."

"Walking in the office Lorenzo took his jacket off and hung it on the back of the chair showing he had a glock 9 on him."

"Mr. Deniro please have a seat and tell me what I can do for you."

"Lorenzo, I would like to clear the air up on a few things."

"I'm listening."

"My family had nothing to do with Marcus and Jamila's problems. When I found out what happened and how he tried to bring my family and the LaCross family to war, I had him killed for that."

"The problem with what you is telling me Mr. Deniro is that Ms. Simpson said she was there when that conversation took place. And you wanted southside Queens and Red Invee and Frankie were in both y'all way."

"Do you mind if I smoke in here Lorenzo?"

"Go ahead," Lorenzo passed him an ashtray across the desk.

"Yes, me and Frankie have our problems that need to be resolved in the streets or out of them, but we do not have a problem with the LaCross family."

"Mr. Deniro, I'm glad to hear that come from your mouth and I will take your word."

"So, we do have an understanding Lorenzo?"

"Yes, we do."

"I will inform Jamila about this meeting. I greatly appreciate you coming down here in person and letting me know that."

"It's what I hope you would do if we had a misunderstanding Lorenzo."

"And I would Mr. Deniro."

"Lorenzo, I have never seen a restaurant like this before it is beautiful inside of here."

"Thank you. Jamila put a lot into this place."

"Where is Jamila? I was hoping to see her this morning."

"She's out of town right now handling some personal business."

After twenty minutes of talking about the restaurant and some future business they may be able to do Mr. Deniro shook hands with Lorenzo and him and Gino left.

Lorenzo asked himself, "Can all this be true or is he just trying to rock me to sleep?"

*****

Two Days Later…

When Jamila returned the very first thing, she did was call Lorenzo and told him to meet her at the office. When Lorenzo arrived, Jamila was on the phone with Ms. Jackson.

"Ms. Jackson let me call you back about that, or I'll come down there and talk to you face to face sometime this afternoon." She hung up the phone.

"How was your trip Jamila?"

"It was too short."

"I know you said you was going to be gone four weeks, but it's been a several days short of that."

"Please don't remind me. I know."

"But I'm glad you are back. Let me fill you in while you were gone."

Jamila got up from her desk and walked to the bar and got a bottle of water and told Lorenzo to come sit on the deck with her. And tell her what she been missing.

"Every time I come on this deck, Jamila, I think about how far we've come."

"And Lorenzo it's only going to get better for us. So, talk to me."

"Well, Deniro came by here with Gino and a few men to talk to me about what happened. He told me his family had no issue with us, but they are at war with Frankie."

"You know what that's good to hear, but we both know that's some bullshit. But we will pay Frankie and Fabio a visit tomorrow and let them know why we are cutting off all ties with them. Lorenzo, I have some calls to make and I will catch up with you in a little while."

"Ok well I'll go by Passions and see Kent. Call me if you need me."

"I will."

When Lorenzo left out the room Jamila got up and locked the door then walked in her bird cage to her office no one knew about. Jamila trusted Lorenzo, but she also knew how the game can turn on you for the worst. She wasn't about to take no risk. She decided not to reach out to Frankie. She didn't want to look the man in the face who been lying to her for the last four years. She knew she couldn't trust him no more. Morwell told her: *you only have one friend and it's your instincts,* and her instinct told her there had been too many lies coming out of Frankie's mouth. She told herself to walk away while she still could.

SAYNOMORE

Chapter Nine

The Next Day…

Jamila went to Destiny's and found Frankie waiting for her there.

"Jamila, can I talk to you for a minute?" Frankie said walking towards her from the bar area.

"I know why you haven't been in touch with me. You felt I betrayed you."

Looking into Jamila's eyes, not saying a word, he knew what he was saying was right.

"Yes, Fabio was alive, and I knew about it and ain't tell you but let me ask you this. If you faked your death and asked me not to tell no one and I did, would you be able to trust me again? I was being loyal to a friend like I been loyal to you for the past four years."

Jamila never saw it that way, but he was right.

"Now can we go somewhere and talk?" he asked. When Jamila nodded her head, he said, "Follow me to the ballroom."

"Okay." She walked behind him.

Sitting down at the table, Frankie said, "Jamila, hear me out."

"Wait, Frankie I understand why you ain't tell me but for the past four years I mourned for this man. I killed people over his death, and it was all a lie. What you are saying is true Frankie I can't be upset at you, but I don't have no words for him at all."

"Jamila, where do we go from here?"

"Yesterday Frankie I went and signed all your business back over to you. I went and did all you asked me to do. That night at the hospital I kept my word to you and never broken it. But right now, I have the FBI watching me and I just want to run my family and make sure all my I's are dotted and T's are crossed before I have a case before me. Fabio is back now he can help you from here on out."

"So, are you telling me this is the end of us?"

"Frankie, I have a lot on my plate right now and I need sometime that's all."

"Jamila, remember years ago I told you I lost two brothers but not to death but rather to a change of heart that loyalty brings upon us? Jamila, have a shot with me.

They walked to the bar and Jamila poured two shots of gin.

"What are we drinking to Frankie?"

"The code of silence."

They took they shots Frankie looked at Jamila and got up and walked out the ballroom.

"Frankie."

"Yes?"

He turned around and looked at Jamila, "the Deniro family are after you. They stopped at Jelani's the other day and told Lorenzo that you have some unfinished business with them. And that it's going to end in the streets so watch your back."

Frankie took a deep breath and walked out the door. He knew Jamila was loyal and knew where her heart was at. He just wished she could have found out another way not like she did.

Jamila watched as he walked out the ballroom.

When Frankie made it outside, Fabio opened the car door for him.

"Frankie how did it go?"

Getting into the car, "Fabio, she is more hurt than anything right now but in time her wounds will heal. Right now, we have a bigger problem to deal with."

"And what's that?" asked Fabio.

"Jamila just told me it's the Deniro family who is after me."

"We know that, but can we take her word?"

"Yes, I can take her word."

"So how do you want to deal with it?"

"First, we won't let him know we know. Never let your right hand know what your left hand is doing. Fabio, I want you to call a meeting with our family."

Riding through the city, Frankie looked out the window at all the businesses. As the car took them back to the Bronx.

"Fabio, I need to know, are you going to war with me?"

"Yea, I'm not leaving no more. I have someone running my establishments for me. So, I only have to go to Paris once a month to show my face."

"Good because from here on out you are my number two."

"With that being said I think we should go straight after him cut the head off and watch the body drop. Put a bomb in his wife car and kill her and the children. Then let him deal with the cards he dealt."

"Fabio, I'm an old man, now I can't move like I use to, so I want you to keep in mind whatever you do just make sure it don't come back on me. I'll let you deal with Mr. Deniro. You have my blessing on whatever you do."

"Thank you, Frankie."

"Fabio, I know you love Jamila but until this war is over, I need you to leave her alone or it might hurt us in the long run."

Fabio looked at Frankie and nodded his head looking out the window.

SAYNOMORE

Chapter Ten

"Take it easy hot stuff we got all night," as La La jumped all over Gino making him fall on the bed.

"Did you bring some candy?"

"Where the fuck did you get this candy shit from?" asked Gino. "Yea I bring some cocaine the good stuff."

Pouring three grams on the nightstand, Gino watched as LaLa buried her nose in it.

"Woo woo damn, that's good stuff."

"I told you I had the good stuff. Now come over here and slid down the pole."

Jumping on the bed LaLa started kissing all over Gino grabbing his dick and placing it in her.

"Damn daddy you got me wet. Smack my ass Gino."

"You been wanting this pipe babe."

Gino pulled her down as he sucked on her titties. "Don't stop keep moving your hips just like that bae." Flipping her over Gino picked her legs up in the air and started pounding her box out.

"Gino no, Gino don't stop, this is your pussy daddy. I'm cumming daddy. Damn Gino. Gino."

"Michael I'm not about to stand at this door and listen to this shit. Let's go downstairs and have a smoke. Pass me one of them, Willy. Word is that Deniro wants to make a move on Frankie this week."

"I heard that too."

"You got a lite Michael?"

"Shit, I left it in the car."

"Willy, watch the front of the house I'll go around back and get it out the car. I'll be right back."

Walking on the side of the house there was a cat that jumped out from behind the trash can making Michael jump.

"Shit, you damn fur ball. I can't believe this shit Deniro got me babysitting his damn cousin," opening the car door reaching in grabbing the lighter out. When he went to close the door, Fabio jammed a knife in his throat pinning him against the car as blood came out of his mouth. He then pulled the knife out and stabbed him in the stomach two times laying his body on the ground. Getting up and pointing two fingers at his man telling him to come on. Looking at Willy, Fabio walked out from the side of the house.

"What the fuck? Who the fuck are you?"

"I'm nobody."

Willy pulled his gun out, but it was too late. He got hit in the back of the head with a brick knocking him out cold.

"Come on help me drag his body to the side of the house."

Gino is still in there wasn't nobody else with them. "He's still alive. What we going to do with him?"

Pulling his knife out Fabio stabbed him in the throat then jammed his knife in his heart.

"Come on now, let's get Gino."

"Hold on bae let me hit a line really quick."

"Put one to the side for me too, Gino." As he rolled up his dollar the room door opened up.

"What's up Gino?"

Gino's eyes got big as hell when he saw Fabio with the gun in his hand.

"What the fuck you want?"

"Frankie sends his regards."

Gino's body hit the floor as Fabio shot him four times in the chest making him fall out the chair. LaLa was screaming. Fabio looked at her and shot her point blank in the head.

"Let's get the fuck out of here. We just sent Mr. Deniro a personal message."

*****

"Hey Boss, I'm sorry for your loss."

Mr. Deniro turned around and looked at Johnny.

"Look at him just laying here. They shot and killed my little cousin four times to the chest." Taking a rag whipping his face off looking at his cousin laying on the cold metal tray in the morgue. "You can cover him back up."

"Johnny come on."

"What you want to do?"

"I want blood for my blood."

"Who you think did it?"

"Frankie's name is on this."

"You sure it wasn't Red Invee?"

"This was personal. Frankie wanted me to know it was him."

Getting in the car he looked at Johnny. "He wants to play let's play. Put a car bomb in his car I want his ass dead. I don't care how it gets done. Just get it done."

*****

Frankie was eating a tomato in his backyard when Fabio walked up.

"I delivered the message to Deniro."

"Good! It doesn't stop now. He has a car wash off of Lincoln Ave. Have it shot up. I want him to feel our pain. Lee goes get the car and I'll be right out front."

"Fabio just know Deniro's not going to lay down so keep your eyes open, if you want to live." Fabio walked to the front of the house and saw a white van parked down the street with two guys in it. He looked at Lee.

"Lee don't, don't Lee," he took off running to the car but was blown back by the car explosion. That's when the van took off speeding towards Fabio. The side door opened up and a masked man was hanging out the door shooting an AK-47 at him. Fabio ran and jumped behind a parked car as the van drove off. His head was ringing as he stood up and saw the car fire and the van turning the corner. Frankie ran to the front of the house, "Where is Lee?"

"Dead, I couldn't get to him in time."

Frankie looked at the car and Lee's body in it.

*****

"Chief Tadem you heard what happened?"

"No."

"Frankie Landon's house was shot up and a car bomb killed one of his guys."

"I'm guessing this is because of Gino, Deniro's cousin who was killed three days ago."

"What he has to say?"

"Code of silence, he knew nothing."

"It's going to get a lot worse before it gets better, Boatman. What can you tell me about Lorenzo?"

"He's clean work and home. We been following him for weeks, phone taps nothing came up."

"Detective, nobody is that good and Jamila?"

"She's been gone for three and a half weeks. I don't know where she went. She's protected by someone because she's always one step ahead of us. We need someone to go undercover and become a part of the LaCross family. We need eyes and ears on the inside."

"Chief Tadem, there's nothing on record that can back my statement up. But there have been rumors of how she killed people for trying her family tying them up to tree and letting the wild dogs eat them sending heads back to love ones. Even putting them on a meat hook. You're asking someone to go undercover in the LaCross family, you're asking them to commit suicide."

"Boatman let me think and I'll get back at you later."

"Ok, Chief Tadem."

*****

Lorenzo walked in Jamila's office. Jamila was outside on her deck talking on the phone with her back turned to him. He made his way to the bar and made a light drink then he took a seat at the table. Hearing the sliding doors close Jamila walked in.

"Lorenzo if it ain't one thing it's another. You should have made me a drink too."

"I did it's right here. What's going on?"

"More money more problems."

"Well, did you hear Frankie's house was attacked and a car bomb killed one of his guys?"

"When this happened?" Jamila asked.

"Yesterday, but three days before that, Deniro's little cousin was killed. Shot four times and the two guys he was with had their throats were cut from ear to ear. The 7 is calling a meeting because they trying to stop this before it gets out of hand."

Taking his sip and placing his glass back on the table.

Walking to the bar Jamila put two ice cubes in her drink. "So, when is this meeting taking place?"

"At 5 tonight".

"Lorenzo when you look out the window, what do you see?"

"I see the city of New York. What you see?"

"My backyard and I think I'm ready to leave the nest."

"Jamila, what are you saying to me?"

"I'm saying we lost friends and loved ones we killed more people than we can count. We went through mob wars and made it out. Lorenzo, how much money do you have in the bank?"

"$4 Million."

"You have $4 million in the bank what more do you need? The ones who stay in this game dies. I'm not ready to die. I'm thinking about selling everything and move someplace else and start over."

"Jamila, I know you are hurt because of what Fabio did to you but running away will not take the pain away. If you truly want to leave, I'm with you. Look I have some runs to make and I'll see you at five for the meeting."

"I'll be ready."

*****

Jamila walked out of Jelani's wearing an all-black suit with her hair pulled to the back and a pair of sunglasses covering her face.

Lorenzo opened the door to the limo for her.

"You ready?"

"Yea, let's get this over with."

"Where is Badii and Young Boy at?"

"Badii is at the Waste Plant and Young Boy is at Destiny's and Muscle is here walking around back right now."

"Ok let's go."

"Jamila you know I hate these meetings."

"I do too, but we have to be there."

As they arrived at the location of the meeting Jamila pulled her gun out and checked it.

"Isn't that Frankie's car over there Jamila?"

"Yea it is he's trying to see who pulling up and what car making sure everything is good, I guess."

"Where is everybody else car?"

"Lorenzo, what time you said this meeting was?"

"At 5."

"Something doesn't feel right."

Johnny looked out the window from across the street.

"They are here Mr. Deniro."

"Set it off."

Johnny pulled out and made a call.

"It's a go."

Looking out the window Deniro had his hands behind his back watching everything.

Frankie's driver opened his door and walked around the limo to open the door for Frankie, a UPS truck came driving down the street. Jamila looked at Lorenzo but before she could say a word all you saw was men jumping out the back of the UPS truck shooting AR15's at Frankie's limo.

"Fabio down, it's a set up."

His driver got hit as the bullets went through his body hitting Frankie's limo.

"Come on Jamila out the limo hurry up."

Two men started shooting AK47's at her limo.

Bullets were ripping holes in the side of her limo as the windows were busted out.

Lorenzo grabbed Jamila and ran inside the building. Jamila looked up and saw a high-powered assault rifle pointed at her. Lorenzo pulled her to the floor as they shot the building up trying to hit them. They pulled her driver out the car and shot him up in front of everybody. Fabio jumped in the driver's seat of the limo and pulled off as they shot it up for three minutes went flying through Frankie and Jamila's limo. Frankie's driver was killed and two of his men. It happened so fast they didn't have time to shot back. Jamila's driver was dead and all you heard was tires peeling off and police sirens approaching.

"Jamila, you okay?"

"I think they are gone."

Jamila started shaking out of control.

"They tried to kill me. Lorenzo, help me up."

Looking out the window it was a mess.

"They set us up Lorenzo."

Glass was everywhere. Looking down on the ground Jamila saw over a thousand bullet casing on the ground. Looking at her driver lying dead in the street next to Frankie's men her limo was shot up too.

"Jamila you are bleeding?"

"It's ok. I cut myself on a piece of glass. Look that's Frankie's limo."

Frankie and Fabio were getting out the limo. Frankie was yelling, "You fucked up, I'm still here. Do you hear me? You fucked up."

Lorenzo had his gun in his hand. Him and Fabio made brief eye contact for a moment. Frankie looked at Jamila and nodded his head at her. When the police pulled up Jamila and Frankie went inside the building before they could be seen Fabio and Lorenzo walked behind them.

"Are you ok Jamila?"

"Yea, I'm fine Frankie."

"Are you ready for this war?"

"Frankie, I thought I was dead. They tried to kill me."

"Me too, Jamila We know what we need to do. You and Fabio need to talk so we can win this war. I need him to have a clear head for this."

Jamila knew deep inside her heart Frankie was right. She had to face the facts they need to talk.

*****

"Mr. Deniro, we shot them limos up. We sprayed a thousand shells at each limo. God must've been with them because they lived."

Mr. Deniro closed his eyes and took a deep breath and said, "I had it set up to kill two birds with one stone."

"How did ya fuck it up?"

"My thoughts on what I wanted to happen kill Frankie and Red Invee at the same damn time at the meeting, but you failed me so now get out leave me."

*****

"This is Barbara Smith with Channel 7 News. Over the last two weeks there has been car bombing shootouts and over thirteen people have been killed. And two unsolved murders from last month that followed a deadly shooting at the hospital. Three police officers were killed this truly is the year death walks the streets of New York City. This is a Mob war like the one we had Four years ago where Mayor Oakland of New York City was killed, and bodies being found in garbage dumpsters and the Hudson river over a turf. Here comes Chief Tadem from the 24th police station."

"Chief Tadem, do you have anything to say about this war on the streets of New York City?"

"I have no comments at this time."

"This leaves one question, who really runs the streets of New York City and when is this war going to end? This is Barbara Smith with Channel 7 Action News signing out.

Chapter Eleven

"Lorenzo, I want this motherfucker dead. I want his blood on the streets." Jamila walked back and forth on her office floor with her black 9 mm in her hand.

"I'm working on that now. Ain't nobody sees him."

"Hold on Lorenzo that's my phone going off."

Picking up the phone she walked out to the deck. "Hello?"

"Hey, look I can't talk long, but I need you to meet someone on 45th street her name is Crystal".

"You will be meeting her from here on out. There's a lot going on I can't talk about right now. She will be waiting on you at the subway. She has a red bag. She will be there in twenty-five minutes."

Hanging up the phone Jamila walked into her office.

"Lorenzo, I have to meet someone I'll be back in a few."

"Do you need me to come with you?"

"No, I got this I'll be fine."

"Please be safe."

"I will."

*****

Jamila walked into the subway on 45th street she saw a white lady with blonde hair and sunglasses on sitting at the back table with a red purse on it. Walking up to the table.

"Crystal?"

"Jamila?"

"Yes, have a seat. Our mutual friend wanted me to meet you from here on out."

"Not to sound rude, but tell me what's going on that I had to meet you as soon as possible?"

Deja and DamarThere's a big case on you, Frankie and Deniro. They know everything not just the FBI but the DEA's involved now on the case. Now they are ready to move in on y'all."

"But Mr. Stone said they didn't have anything on us!"

"It's a secret indictment. He had no idea they were working on it."

"How long do we have?" Jamila asked.

"Two or three days at the most. Jatavious just found out within the last hour. There's a lot of heat up there where he's at right now. Look Jamila on 127th street is where your cases and all photos of y'all are being held. There are agents there 24/7."

"What are you trying to tell me?"

"If that building blows up, so do your cases, but hear me well. It will bring more heat on you than ever before if it comes back that you did it."

"What's the address?"

"66 127th Street."

"Thank you."

"Wait, I have one more thing for you. 134th suite twenty-three is where a large shipment of cocaine is being held from a bust five months ago."

"I know what you are talking about."

"Good, it's the fourth building on the right."

"Crystal, thank you!"

"You're welcome Jamila."

Jamila got up and walked off and called Lorenzo. "Set up a meeting with Frankie and have him meet us at Destiny's within the hour." When Jamila pulled up, she saw Frankie and Fabio walking into Destiny's with Lorenzo. As Jamila walked in Destiny's she walked up to Frankie at the bar. Nobody was in there but them four.

"I just had a meeting with my sources. They just told me the FBI and DEA involved now and they plan on moving in on us in two to three days from now. Not just us but the Deniro family too."

"I knew this was coming," Frankie said looking around.

"Wait Frankie there's more, they gave me the information to where our cases are being held. And they said if the building blows up so do our cases."

"Well let's blow that motherfucker up then."

"They also said it will bring more heat on us than ever before."

Frankie took a rag and wiped his forehead off.

"Jamila, Fabio listen to me blow that bitch up and we will cross that bridge when we get there. I'm trying to kill this snake and stay out of prison."

"Lorenzo, do you still have your people that can take care of this problem for us?"

"Yeah, Jamila I do."

"Good go sees them and have them blow the building up at 3 am."

"Frankie, do you think you can find out where Deniro lives at?"

"I don't know I can try. I'm not promising you nothing. Why you want to know where he lives?"

"C4 to his front door and two birds got killed with one stone."

"Jamila, I know how you like to move but it's just not him there."

"And Frankie if he sends word by whoever he sends will put a bullet in our forehead if they had the chance so fuck them too."

"Jamila, everyone doesn't have to die."

"Frankie, I think you getting shot made you weak."

"Jamila, if you kill them you are weaker and power hungry. There's only one person who needs to die and the rest will lay down, Jamila. But, I'll let the ball roll the way you want it to roll. Just know every family have one backing them up just like I did with you when you started."

"Yeah, Frankie just like Tony had Sammy who had Sunnie who had Alex. and since you want to bring up families backing others up. Did they lie to them too?"

"Jamila, I see you still have a lot on your chest but for us to get through this we need to move as one. So, let's just put everything on the table now."

"There's nothing to put on the table."

"Wait Frankie, she's upset at me. Jamila, I did what I did. I can't take it back but I'm trying to get past this with you."

"You want to get past this Fabio? Bring back Isaiah back from the dead or Nayana back who I killed over you. You think because you are here now that that shit means something to me now? Where was you when I got shot? Sleeping peaceful. Miss me Fabio with the bullshit."

"Jamila who the fuck you think you talking to? I ain't no weak ass nigga."

"Shit you could've fooled the fuck out of me. Your heart went from brave to bitch when it was crunch time. But you know what, I killed the motherfuckers who killed your family. I stayed ten toes down, I popped the bottle. Where was you at?"

Fabio shook his head, "Jamila can we talk in private please?"

Looking at Lorenzo she knew he was ready to kill for her. "Lorenzo can you please go take care of that for me."

"You going to be good?"

"Yea I am. You have one minute Fabio what's up?"

"Jamila who are you? This is not the female I fell in love with."

"You can't be for real. Did you just say that to me? I might be a little out of line, but you left me to die. I been shot. My friends are dead, and I don't have a reason to be upset. Fabio after this is over, stay the fuck out my life or I'll kill you myself and you won't come back from the dead. I promise you that." Jamila glared at Fabio and walked out the door.

*****

Jamila sat down drinking more than she normally does with a thousand thoughts running through her mind. She was stuck between love and anger, hate and trust for concerns she couldn't get passed a nightmare. She saw Nayana's lifeless body. The look flashed back on her when she shot her. Sitting at the table she picked the bottle of Cîroc up and took a long shot. Walking out her front door she got in her car and drove off. Parking across the street from Deniro's pool hall pulling her glock 9 out she took another shot out the bottle. Everything she saw was double vision to her.

"Johnny, what time we going to see Mr. Deniro?"

"He wants us at the house by 10:30 tonight, Blue."

"Shit we might as well leave now." Slapping a $20 bill on the bar, Johnny and Blue walked out.

"You think this is over the hit that we missed?"

"The fuck if I know, Blue." Opening the pool hall door.

Jamila looked at both of them. Pulling out the parking lot from across the street she rolled her window down.

"Excuse me, I'm looking for Mr. Deniro."

"Who the fuck are you?" said Blue walking to the car before they realized who she was. Jamila pointed her gun at them and shot Blue two times in the chest, dropping him. Johnny pulled his gun out and dropped it as he tripped over his feet. Jamila jumped out of the car.

"Don't do it," said Johnny.

"See, that pussy got you killed, Mr. Deniro." Jamila pointed the gun at his forehead. All he saw was a spark as she emptied the clip in his face running back to the car she peeled off.

*****

Walking into the hole in the wall strip club, Lorenzo sat in the back.

"Hey handsome, can I get you something to drink?"

Looking at the waitress beautiful body half-dressed he pulled out $100 bill.

"Yeah, beautiful let me get a double shot of Cîroc and you see that man over there in the corner with the blue shirt on. Let him know I need to talk to him, and you can keep the change," watching her walk away Lorenzo turned his eyes to the stage looking at the sexy young girl dancing on the pole to Usher and Jeezy's song *Love In The Club*.

"Excuse me sir."

"Yeah cutie."

"That man in the corner asked me to tell you to come see him."

Looking at Lorenzo he shook his head.

"Thank you."

Picking his glass up walking over there to his through the crowd of people on the floor.

"Lorenzo, it's been a while."

"I know Avon."

"You coming to find me in this place just tell me you need something."

"You know me too well. Let's talk outside."

The waiter brought Lorenzo his drink he took the shot and walked outside with Avon.

Lorenzo opened his car door. "Get in."

"Nice car."

"Thank you."

"So, what you need Lorenzo?"

"I need a building gone yesterday."

"I got something that will blow up a block. But you need a building."

Avon wasn't a drug dealer or a gang banger. He just knew how to make bombs and was good at it.

"How much Avon?"

"$20,000 plus $5,000."

"What's the $5,000 for?" Lorenzo asked.

"Because I'm the only one who can set it up."

"How long will it take you to set it up?"

"Fifteen to thirty minutes, the most give or take."

"What if I said I need it done tonight?"

"I'll say let's go."

"Good because I need it done tonight."

"Just give me the address."

"I'm coming with you this has to be done right."

"Where is this place at?" Avon asked.

"It's the FBI Headquarters off of 47th street."

"Come on let's get everything ready."

"This got to be done by 3 a.m." Lorenzo started the car up and drove off.

*****

Simeon ran out the pool hall with his gun in his hand just in time to see the black BMW speed off.

"Fuck damn Johnny," he put his hands on his head and closed his eyes looking at Johnny laying there dying. He looked at Blue then heard him cough. He ran to him picking his head up and wiping the blood from his mouth as Blue tried to talk.

"Don't say nothing. Try to keep your energy. Call 911, get some help hurry up," Simeon yelled back in the pool hall.

In a very weak voice Simeon, "it was Red Invee."

"Don't worry about that now. I'm here help is on the way. You going to be just fine. Just stay with me. Keep your eyes open."

Simeon was holding his head trying to keep him from choking on his blood. With one more cough of blood out his mouth, Blue was dead. Simeon laid his head down and closed Blue's eyes. Getting up looking at pain with Blue's blood on his hand and shirt.

"Go call Mr. Deniro and let him know we was just hit at the pool hall and Red Invee killed Johnny and Blue."

*****

"You fucked up Jamila LaCross I got you now. Four years no slip ups till now." Detective Boatman said as he watched Jamila kill Johnny and Blue. He took pictures of everything.

Jamila was so out of her mind from drinking the Cîroc she ain't notice the blue town car following her from her house.

"I told you one day Johnny someone was going to clap your ass. I'm just glad I was able to see it happen. Your life just gave me a gold mine. Now you have to pay the piper, Ms. LaCross," pulling up to the 7-11 Detective Carter was walking out.

"Detective Boatman, funny seeing you out this time of night."

"Yea, you know how them stakeouts go."

"Who the fuck you are staking out?"

"Jamila LaCross."

"Shit give that one up. I had her under investigation for two years day and night stakeouts and ain't shit come up on her."

Picking up his camera, Boatman smiled.

"What you got there?" Carter said with a curious look on his face.

"A goldmine full of diamonds."

"What are you talking about, Boatman?"

"Shit follow me to my house and I'll show you but first let me get a cup of coffee out of here."

"Boatman your ass had me follow you way over here to show me what?"

"Come in and closed the door behind you."

"What is all of this?"

"Take a seat. So Chief Tadem had me follow Jamila for the last five months. Tonight, I followed her to Mr. Deniro's poolhall off of Bayview. There was an abandoned building there, so I set up my stake out inside. Now, I saw two guys coming out the pool hall. I knew one of them as Johnny Deniro. I couldn't tell who the other guy was. It was dark I couldn't see his face. That's when I saw a black BMW pull up."

"Who was in the black BMW?"

"The one and only Jamila LaCross. So, let me finish. The one guy walked up to her car and that's when I saw and heard two-gun shots. I saw Johnny fall down. That's when she got out the car and shot him in the face five times. She ran back in her car and drove off."

"Can you prove all of this?"

"I got pictures of everything from Jamila standing over his body shooting him point blank range in the face."

"You got to be kidding me. Jamila LaCross. The one who donated money to the Stop the Crime foundation after the Mayor was killed. I remember following her and Chris to the Mayor's ball. Her and Jatavious Stone took a picture together that night. She is a big public figure in New York City. This is a big bust."

"Check the pictures out."

Carter was looking at the digital photos of Jamila killing both men. Carter's eyes got big.

"Fuck me. When did this happen?"

"Not even an hour ago."

"What the fuck Boatman, I just heard this call over the radio not even an hour ago. We need to call this in and let the Cheif know what we got."

"Hold on, Carter think big we can get an easy $20,000 a month for these pictures from her."

"Look Boatman I'm not with that. That shit can blow up in our face and bite us in the ass. I'm not down. I'm a cop first, and if you don't report this then I will."

"You know what you're right Carter. Take the camera and I'll meet you at the car."

"Now you are thinking," grabbing the camera and turning around walking towards the door Boatman shot him in the back of the head killing him.

"Fuck what you are talking about Carter now you dead and I'll take that camera back. Thank you."

*****

"We made our point tonight to Frankie and Red Invee. We will not go out like the Lenacci family," said Ricky, smoking his cigar and looking out the window at the lake behind his house. "You know it would have been beautiful to have both their bodies in a watery grave in that lake back there tied to some bricks underwater."

"We almost had them today Mr. Deniro and we sent three of the guys swimming with the fishes." There was a knock at the door, turning around blowing smoke out of his mouth.

"Come in."

"Excuse me Mr. Deniro."

"What is it cutie?"

"I just got a phone call from Lue the poolhall was hit. Johnny and Blue are dead. It was Red Invee."

"When the fuck did this happen?"

"Just now boss."

Walking to his desk and knocking everything off and kicking his chair over. "I want this bitch fucking dead, dead you hear me?"

"Boss, I know where they are."

"You know where the fuck they are at?"

"Yes."

"Go kill them and if they live, you are fucking dead. Bring me that bitch head back. Now get the fuck out."

"Boss I'll go down to the pool hall and see what happened down there. I'll be back."

Mr. Deniro ain't say a word he just looked at Ricky walking out the door. Then he got up and looked at the lake behind his house.

*****

Jamila pulled up at Frankie's house and got out with the bottle of Cîroc in her hand and leaned against her car taking another shot out the bottle.

Opening the front door Frankie walked outside to Jamila.

"It's late is everything alright?" Looking around his yard. Are you drunk?"

"No, Frankie, I'm not drunk. I have been drinking."

Placing his hand on her shoulder.

"Wait Frankie, there's something I have to say to you. I know you would never betray me, and you did what you thought was best for Fabio you ain't know me at the time. So, keeping his secret was being loyal to him. I respect that Frankie."

"So why are you making it so hard on Fabio?"

"Because he left me, and I will never trust him again. He should have stayed with me and bled in these streets with me, but I did it without him."

"Jamila, go talk to Fabio he is very hurt over this."

"I will in time but right now I need to show you something. Don't look at me like that Frankie. I know you would never let anything happen to me. But let me show you something."

"And what is that?"

"Come take a ride with me Frankie I'm sorry for not understanding your loyalty to Fabio, to a friend."

"Why are you here and not at the house I put you in?"

"I ain't think you wanted me there. Let me go get Fabio, pull up around back. We will take the back way out."

Jamila picked up the phone and called Lorenzo.

"Jamila, what's up?"

"Meet us at the pond. How are things going over there?"

"He's setting it up now it should be ready in five minutes."

"Can he hear me?" asked Jamila.

"No."

"Give him the chance to come to our family tonight. If he says no, then I don't want no witnesses you understand me?"

"Yea I do, and I'll meet you at the pond when I'm done here."

"Frankie and Fabio coming out. I'll see you back at the pond."

"Jamila how far is this place?"

"Twenty minutes from here."

"Jamila you want me to drive?"

"No Fabio, I got this. Thanks though."

They pulled up to a little log house with a pond on the side of the house.

"Jamila, what is this place?"

"The pond. Frankie, come inside. I have to show you something."

Looking at Fabio as he walked downstairs to the cellar. Frankie ain't no what to expect. "It's in this room Frankie."

Opening the door, Frankie was shocked to see all his cocaine he lost six months ago to the New Jersey police when they hit his shipment and seized his shit.

"Jamila, how and when did you get it back?"

"A few hours ago, but you know that's the last question I'll answer about that." Frankie knew she couldn't tell her source. Lorenzo pulled up to the house and saw Jamila talking to Frankie out front of the house next to the pond. He walked up to both of them, "it's done the building is in smoke and two more next to it."

"And what about our friend?"

"He's a part of our family now."

"Good."

"I see you showed Frankie the good news."

"Yea, I did."

"Jamila who else know about this place?"

"Nobody, Frankie just us."

"Let's stay here tonight. It's already 3 am let's let the sunrises before we leave. Come on let's go inside.

*****

"Do you think they still in there?"

"Yea they are Red Invee just pulled up. She was outside talking to Frankie I had someone watching the house."

"Ken Ken where they at?"

"Frankie just went back inside ten minutes ago and Red Invee pulled up around back."

"Get ready on my count we going to light this bitch up."

Cutie had a five-man team outside of Frankie's house.

Putting his hand up showing five fingers.

Five, four, three, two, one. They started shooting 500 rounds per minute. It sounded like World War 2 out there. The windows were broken out and the side of the house fell in. Cutie signaled one of his men now he threw two grenades in the house watching the house blow up. Smoke and fire were two stories high was all you saw.

"Come on let's get the fuck out of here."

They got in the cars and drove off. "Call Mr. Deniro and tell him it's done. That itch is taking care of."

*****

Jatavious was in the kitchen eating at the table watching the news.

Breaking news downtown on 47th street a building was bombed, killing four FBI agents and two DEA agents that were inside working on a case. They had been investigating for the last seven months. We don't know the details of the case that is confidential. From what we are being told the bombs went off around 4:30 this morning blowing up three buildings. As you could see behind me thick gray smoke that filled the air. There are seven fire trucks down there fighting fire down and looking for any more people who could have been inside one of these buildings. Also, in Long Island Mob Boss, Frankie Landon's house was shot up with multiple rounds then blew up afterwards. No one was hurt but four weeks earlier a car bomb killed one man at Mafia boss Frankie Landon's house after it was shot up. "Could there be a connection somehow This is Barbara Smith with Channel 7 Action news signing out.

Jatavious cut the TV off.

"I guess Deniro just won't give up and I hope Red Invee know what she just did. Let me get down there to show my face," Jatavious said to himself.

*****

Jamila walked downstairs to the cellar where Frankie and Lorenzo were. They were counting up all Frankie's cocaine. Taking a seat on the wooded steps in the cellar. Frankie walked up to her.

"What's wrong Red Invee?"

"Your house was being watched last night. It's all over the news, they shot it up and set it on fire. I just saw what's left of your house on the news. If I would have never came and got you, you and Fabio would have been killed last night."

"It's good I had everything moved out that house into the house you got me a few weeks ago."

"As far as our case go, it's over with. The building went up in flames and five agents were killed."

"Red Invee we might still be under investigation. I don't want to take no risk of moving any of this right now."

"It's safe here. Don't nobody know about this house. I'm about to go home and shower then head to Jelani's. Lorenzo, what are you about to do?"

"I'm staying here and help Frankie and Fabio out. I'll catch up with you later."

Getting up Red Invee started walking up the stairs.

"Jamila."

"Yeah, Lorenzo."

"Be safe."

"I will be trust me. I'll see you at the restaurant."

*****

With two stress balls in his hand, Deniro was sitting down on his desk talking to Rickey when Cuttie walked in.

"Cuttie you told me you knew where they were at you said you had a man watching the house. See I been watching the news all morning and I heard them say 4 FBI agents and two DEA agents was killed in a bombing this morning. That's good because all pigs should die. They also said Mob boss Frankie Landon's house was shot up, but nobody was killed." Getting off his desk walking up to Cuttie, "What you have to say about that?"

"I had a guy and he told me they were in the house."

"But there wasn't nobody inside now was it?"

"No boss."

"So how do you think that made me feel? I'm putting my trust in you and you letting me down. Right now, in Red Invee's mind she is winning. In Frankie's mind he is winning too. Johnny and Blue are dead. Both of them got killed last night. You came and told me that. You also said you could take care of Frankie and Red Invee. I said I was going to kill you but I'm not. I'm going to give you a chance to clean your face up with me and show me you ain't no fuck up and kill one of the three, Frankie, Fabio or Red Invee. Walk with me to this window. You see that lake out there?"

"Yea."

"Good because if you fuck up that's where your body will be swimming with the fishes, I promise you that Cuttie." Smacking him two times lightly on the cheek. "Now go."

"Ricky if he fucks up kill him and dump his body in that lake with two bricks tied to his ass. Give him seventy-two hours to get it done. I don't care if he got to run in there with a damn bomb tied to his chest to kill the mother fucker as long as he gets it done."

SAYNOMORE

Chapter Twelve

"Welcome to Jelani's! Will you be eating alone today?"

"No, I came to talk to Ms. Jamila LaCross."

"Do you have an appointment?"

"No, I don't. Can you let her know Detective Boatman is here and needs to have a word with her?"

"Hold on please, I'll let her know Detective Boatman."

Jamila was on her deck looking over the city of Queens. When her phone went off.

"Hello Ms. LaCross speaking."

"Hello Ms. LaCross, this is the front desk. You have a Detective Boatman here to see you. He said he need to have a word with you."

"Let him know I will be right down."

"Yes, Ms. LaCross."

Detective Boatman was looking at her the whole time. "Detective she said she will be right down."

"Thank you."

"You're welcome Detective."

Walking through the lobby Jamila saw Detective Boatman at the front desk looking around. Walking up to him, "Hello Detective Boatman?"

"Yes."

"How are you doing Detective? you needed to talk with me?"

"Yes, I do. Can we go somewhere and talk in private?"

"Yes, follow me to my office."

"You have a beautiful place here."

"Thank you. Come in here and please have a seat."

"So, what can I do for you Detective Boatman?"

"Jamila LaCross I'll get to the point. You fucked up and fumbled the ball. And it's going to cost you. You're going to have to pay the piper."

Crossing her hands, she looked at Detective Boatman and said, "Enlighten me please. And tell me what you are talking about?"

"Here. Have a look at a few of these," as he reached in his top pocket and pulled out a white envelope and passed it to her. Looking at the pictures of her killing Johnny and Blue last night. Staring at the pictures all she could do is smile and shake her head. She passed them back across her desks.

"How much is this going to cost me? To go away?"

"I'm thinking $20,000 a month."

"So, you are bullying me now?"

"No, it's good business. I have you dead to the wrong. You are looking at life if not the needle, so $20,000 should not be a big deal to you. And I would like this to stay between us. No one else has to know. You can keep these copies. I have more plus the video."

Jamila took the pictures and walked back to Detective Boatman.

"I agree to your terms but if you change them and these pictures get out, I'll promise you will bury your fucking mother or whoever you love."

Detective Boatman shook his head to agree.

"I'm glad you agree Detective. Hold on one second," picking up her office phone.

"Hello."

"Tammy would you be a doll and bring me up $40,000? Thank you, Hun."

"Ms. LaCross we all get paid one way or another. I have no ill will with you." Just then there was a knock at the door.

"Hold that thought Detective."

As Jamila went to the door.

"Thank you, Tammy. Detective here is $40,000. From here on out you will not meet up with me but someone from my family who I trust. Today is June 20. So, I don't want to hear from you until August. And you can meet up at my night club Passions at 10 p.m. No one will know about this meeting and remember what we talked about. We stand on our word."

"I won't. Ms. LaCross take care."

"You too, Detective Boatman."

When Detective Boatman left Jamila slammed her fist on her desk and yelled, "Fuck, fuck, fuck." Lorenzo walked in Jamila's office.

"Jamila are you alright? I just saw a Detective coming from out of here."

"Lorenzo that's a story for another day. I just found out last night Deniro's pool hall was hit and two of his guys are dead."

"I know about that already. What is Frankie and Fabio doing?"

"I took them back to the other house this morning, now I'm here."

"Look stay low and watch everything you do. Everything stops till I say different."

"Jamila what's going on?"

"Lorenzo let me just think and I'll talk about it later with you."

"Ok. I'll go check the numbers on all the businesses and I'll let you know how we are doing."

"Thanks Lorenzo!"

*****

Tommy was reading the newspaper in the corner of the room. He had his legs crossed and drinking a cup of coffee smoking a cigarette. The night club was empty but then the men Tommy had walking around. Frankie and Fabio walked through the doors and was stopped at the front.

"Mr. Landon hold on let me let Tommy know you are here."

"Tell him I need to speak with him."

"Frankie this place changed."

"A lot has changed since you been gone Fabio. This is all Tommy's turf now. Since Sammy set up the assassination on the 7 four years ago and Benny Scott was killed. Tommy was the second in line."

Walking back up to Frankie and Fabio. "Landon, he said come on back." Listening to the soft music playing as they walked through the club.

"Tommy."

"Frankie," Tommy said as he got up shook Frankie and Fabio hand.

"Fabio, I heard you was alive. At first, I couldn't go for it. Now seeing is believing."

"Yea, I'm still here."

"Frankie, Fabio have a seat. Frankie, what can I do for you?"

"Tommy it's hard for me to move anything with this disagreement me and Deniro is having right now. So, I'm reaching my hand out to you right now for help."

"Frankie when I first heard you got shot six times, I just knew you was dead. And when I found out who was behind it, I just knew Deniro was dead too. Frankie, we have been friends for a long time, and you have always been loyal. So, I can't tell you no. This is your first time ever asking for a favor all the years I have known you. So, tell me what I can do for you?"

"I need to know where Deniro is at. I need to put a fucking bullet in his head."

Pulling his cigarette Tommy looked at Frankie and Fabio.

"Deniro's at the Lake house in Long Island. Frankie you ain't hear that from me. I don't know what you are talking about. Frankie before you go word is the other night Red Invee knocked two more of Deniro's guys off Johnny and Blue. Got them at the pool hall walking out."

"Where did you hear this from?"

"One of the guys that was there. She's playing for keeps Frankie. We all know what happened to the Lenacci family and how Tony, Sammy, Alex was killed. And still to this day nobody knows what happened to Sunnie. You got a loyal one Frankie don't lose her."

"I don't trust niggas, but she is different."

Getting up from the table. "Tommy, thanks and I won't lose her."

"Fabio good to see you again take care."

"You too Tommy!"

Walking back outside to the limo once inside Frankie pulled out a cigar and lit it.

"Frankie what happened to Sunnie?"

Looking at Fabio Frankie said, "it was bloody and messy. It ended with two bullets to his head. Fabio, Red Invee is very dangerous," pulling his cigar turning his head after them words.

*****

Cutie watched as Jamila walked into Destiny's from across the street with Lorenzo.

"Mrs. Jackson, how are you doing today?"

"I'm fine, Ms. LaCross."

"Can you have the Cheif make up a lunch tray for five and bring it to the ballroom, please?"

"Right away Ms. LaCross."

"Thank you."

"Lorenzo, where is Young Boy, Badii and Muscle at?"

"They should be on the way now."

Walking into Destiny's, Cutie stopped at the front desk.

"Hello. May I help you?"

"I'm looking for Ms. LaCross I just saw her come inside."

"Yes, she went into the ballroom. It's the room on the right."

"Thanks."

"What we need to do is re-open shop. It's been a few weeks and a lot has cooled down."

"Ok Lorenzo. Have Badii and Muscle set shop back up at the Waste Plant, and Young Boy watching the doors."

That's when they both looked at the ballroom door opening and Cutie was standing there looking at both of them.

"I just came to talk nothing else," he said as he walked to Lorenzo and Jamila with both is hands in the air.

"Lorenzo pat him down."

"He's clean."

"Have a seat Mr. Cutie."

"Mr. Cutie you don't have no weapons on you. And you came alone that tell me one or two things. One you fucked up somewhere down the line. Or two you have some information for me, and I can always use information."

"I know how this war is going to end already. And I was told I have seventy-two hours to kill you, Frankie or Fabio. I just don't respect the fact. While we in the field Mr. Deniro is in his lake house in Long Island."

"So, you came to me why Mr. Cutie?"

"To see if you had room in your family for another guy."

The ballroom door opened and Badii, Young Boy and Muscle walked in and Cutie looked at them.

"Look at me Mr. Cutie see here's the thing, how I know you ain't setting me up to kill me?"

"I'm not. I need you to take my word."

Reaching in her purse pulling out a pink and gold 9mm getting up.

"Take your word. You are a fucking trader and a rat. I don't want to take your word. You can't be trusted. You have no fuckin loyalty."

With three pulls of the trigger Cutie's lifeless body was on the floor. Lorenzo jumped back as Jamila shot him. "Damn Jamila, low key we could have used him."

"How the fuck we going to use him Lorenzo? Let me say this to all of you this one time. A snitch and a rat are not the same thing. A snitch is someone minding someone else's business, just like a witness. A fucking rat is a trader. He betrays the trust of his team, his family, to save his ass. And I don't have no place in this family for one. I hope you all understand that." Jamila sat down looking at everyone.

*****

Detective Boatman walked up to the crime scene. "What we got here?"

"A John Doe shot three times in the chest. He wasn't killed here. His body was dumped here." Kneeling, Detective Boatman looked at his face. "This guy Cutie Deniro from the Deniro family. He had this in his mouth, Detective."

Getting up looking at the piece of paper. "The seventy-two-hour deadline expired."

"Well, he had seventy-two hours to do something and missed his deadline. Get him bagged and tagged. I think it's about time I go pay Mr. Deniro a visit because these holes came from the Deniro family or the LaCross family. But somebody made a point."

Walking off back to his car fifteen minutes later walking in the pool hall Detective Boatman took off his sunglasses at the door. Looking around he opened his jacket showing off his badge on his waist as he walked up to the bar looking around at everyone playing pool smoking and drinking.

"What can I do for you?"

"A double shot of gin and tell Mr. Deniro, Detective Boatman is here to see him."

"Here's your drink. I'll be right back." Walking in the back room, "Mr. Deniro you have a Detective Boatman here to see you."

"What the fuck a man can't even smoke a cigar in his own fucking pool hall without the flat foots coming to see him?"

Fixing his tie, he walked to his desk and took a seat. "Go bring him back here. Let me hear what he has to say."

Detective Boatman walked in the backroom looking at Rickey posted up on the wall and Mr. Deniro seated behind his desk.

"So, what do I owe the pleasure of New York City's finest to come visit me?"

"Have a seat Detective. Cigar?"

"No, thanks. Let me get to the point. Mr. Deniro it seems to me your guys are dropping off left and right."

"Is that so Detective Boatman?"

"Yea, it is," crossing his leg.

"Now, I ran across one of your guys about forty-five minutes ago. A Mr. Cutie," reaching in his pocket pulling out a pack of cigarettes and taking one out lighting it.

Deniro looked at Rickey and back at Detective Boatman.

"He was shot three times in the chest and his body was dumped under the train tracks. He also had a note in his mouth. The 72-hour deadline expired. See, I'm not down here to shake you down. I don't give a fuck if you kill every fucking LaCross there is. Or if they kill every fucking Deniro there is, but I can help for a fee every month of $15,000. And if I have to let's say get my hands really dirty, we are talking $30,000."

"And why do I need you?" asked Deniro

"You need eyes and ears where you can't go on both sides of the law. That's where I come in at." Pulling his cigarette leaning back in his chair looking at Deniro's face.

"Ok Detective, I'll play ball. Rickey gets the nice Detective his money. Now what are the terms of this agreement?"

"You are covered and if need be like I said $30,000 and your problem is gone."

"What about Red Invee?"

"Who is Red Invee?" replied Detective Boatman.

"If you don't know who Red Invee is, I might be paying the wrong Detective. Red Invee is Jamila LaCross. I can't put my hands on her. She is paying heavy right now."

"She is safe, I can't put my hands on her. But if one of your guys kills her, I have nothing to do with that."

Ricky handed Deniro $15,000 in a white envelope. "Here you go Detective," handing the money over to Detective Boatman. He looked inside and passed Deniro his card.

"Here is my card if you need to reach me."

Placing the envelope in his top right pocket he got up and walked out the room not looking back. "Rickey, I don't trust that son of a bitch but only time will tell. And find out who knocked Cutie off."

*****

"I called everyone here because I want to thank all of you for your loyalty to the Landon family to each other. It's been a hard year from shoot outs to the loss of family members, but I promise you this will be over soon. From this point on Fabio is my number two in command. And Mickey is my third. Deniro has a nightclub downtown Manhattan. I want it shot up inside and outside and I want security at every one of our spots doubled up. Mickey takes care of that for me. Fabio get everyone where they need to be as far as security goes. The Landon family been running the Bronx for the last twenty years and it's time they feel our pain again. Deniro has a house in Long Island he's been hiding at. We're going to pay him a visit there too. But tonight, Mickey, the club and Fabio, the security. I want bodies in black bags tonight. We are playing dirty, car bombs, house fires, bodies hanging off bridges and in trunks of cars. These motherfuckers want to play ball. Let's play."

Fabio walked outside the meat market talking to Frankie's guys, "from here on out I want to double the security. Shit is about to get really thick. If they are not our family and you see them over here kill them. You see the pole; I want cameras up over there on that pole and over here in front of the store. All sells go to the back door. Trust no one who ain't one of us."

When Fabio turned his back a car was speeding down the street. "Watch out, Fabio."

Guns were hanging out the car as they shot up the meat market. Fabio hit the ground as his men shot back at the car as it was turning the corner.

"Fabio you hit?" He helped him off the ground.

"No, I'm good. Where the fuck that car come from?" Everyone got back inside.

"Shit, shit," Fabio was looking at the broken glass from the front window.

"Get someone in the front and someone get Frankie on the phone now."

SAYNOMORE

Chapter Thirteen

Jamila was in her office watching the news as they talked about all the murders in NYC. Bodies were found in the Hudson River to back alleys, behind buildings. Car bombings and shoot outs, bodies being hung off the bridge. Innocent victims' lives being taken. The news was calling this the devils playground asking the one question, "Is it safe to be outside?"

Jamila respected Deniro because how he moved, he wasn't messy and how he moved not like Sammy or Sunnie. Even Alex never went to the same place twice. Since the war started and he knew where to post his guys up at. And he killed just as many men of her and Frankie's as they killed of his. She needed to get him out somehow. She had the lake house shot up and killed two of his guys, but he wasn't there. He even stopped going to the pool hall. She told Frankie to pull his men back, but he refused, and it cost them their lives. They got caught slipping and was beheaded and then hung off the bridge. It was a matter of time before the FEDS or DEA pick up the case again. They been looking down on the city since the bombing and Deniro was the key to it all. Kill the king and the troops will fall. There are no rules in war Jamila said to herself looking at the city of Queens from her office window. She walked back to her desk and picked up the phone to call Crystal. It was time to bend the rules before she gets life in prison or ends up 6 ft deep.

"Mr. Deniro, I just got word it was Mickey who had the night club shot up." Turning around in his chair tapping his fingers together looking at Ricky."

"You know Ricky, it's time that Detective Boatman puts some work in. Give him a call and tell him Mickey needs to be swimming with the fishes. Getting up looking at the Penthouse window in Manhattan. After he gets done with Mickey let him know Frankie is next. Before you leave call, Vinnie and let him know I would like to have a word with him."

"Sure, thing Boss and when would you like to talk to him?"

"Thursday."

"I'll make the call."

*****

"Ah ah new guy come here. You see this parking spot here?"

"Yea."

"Right here?"

"Yea Mr. Mickey."

"Don't let nobody park here. It's my parking spot you understand me?"

"Yes sir."

"I'll be back in a few, I got to run up the block."

"Yo Mickey where you headed?"

"To pick Jenny up from her mother's then drop her off at her brother's house. I'll be back in thirty minutes, Paul."

Getting in his car pulling off, ten minutes later he pulled up to a brownstone and beeped his horn twice, to see Jenny coming down the stairs. Jumping out to open the door for her.

"Hey bae, what took you so long to come get me?"

"I'm the only one at the bar, I left the new kid and Paul there, so I got to hurry up and get back there. How's your mom?"

"She's fine, she asked about you. Mickey, I feel like I don't even see you no more."

"Jenny. Bae, you know with all this bullshit I don't want you at the bar like that until things cool down Jenny it's for your safety."

"I know bae it's just hard not being around you. My brother's house is right over there bae, pull over. Mickey, what time you going to come back and get me?"

"In a few hours, bae, before 1 am."

"You promise?"

"Yea, I do. Now come on Jenny I have to go, give me a kiss?"

Making a U-turn on the block then the first left as he passed the 7/11, he got pulled over.

"Fuck, what the fuck do these pigs want?"

"Sir, roll your window down and let me see your driver's license and registration."

"For what?" His voice was full of agitation, which caused the cop to respond aggressively.

"Just do as I say!"

"Okay, here you go, officer?" He got his papers out of the glove compartment and handed them over.

"I need you to step out the car and put your hands on the hood, sir."

"What's all this for?" asked Mickey, as he complied.

"You made an illegal U-turn back there." The policeman searched his pockets, then said. "Wait, this is not your day. This looks like two grams of cocaine."

"You got to be fucking kidding me."

"Put your hands behind your back, sir."

"Are you for real?"

"Yes, I am."

"Walk this way," placing Mickey in the back seat of the car.

"When did Detectives start pulling cars over? You might as well be a flashlight cop."

Looking around Detective Boatman said, "I pulled you over because I have a message for you from Mr. Deniro." Mickey's eyes got big as hell as Detective Boatman pulled his gun out and shot him twice in the head while he was handcuffed in the back seat. "MESSAGE DELIVERED!"

*****

It was pouring down rain Jamila had on a black trench coat with a black hat to match holding up an umbrella as her, Lorenzo and Young Boy walked up to Frankie and Fabio with the guys around them in the cemetery.

"Frankie, how are you?"

"Good Jamila. Word is it was a cop who killed him and dumped his body in the Hudson River. Deniro is paying cops to do his dirty work so now we don't know who is whom."

Fabio was looking at everything surrounding them as all of them stood in the rain as Frankie and Jamila talked on top of the hill next to Mickey's grave.

"Frankie, I have a plan to end all of this!"

"And what is that?"

"I'll set up a meeting with him."

"He's not going to go for it, Jamila. He will have a bullet in your head before you know it."

"I got this Frankie," said Jamila as she kissed him on the cheek and dropped a white rose in Mickey's grave walking back down the hill.

"Frankie, what you think about what she just said?"

"I don't know what to think Fabio but, why would you want to talk to the man whose been killing off both of our men? It just doesn't make since or add up to me right now. Come on let's go."

Jamila looked back up the hill at Fabio and Frankie. Fabio looked at her as she was getting back in the limo before catching up with Frankie.

*****

Jamila looked out the window and was thinking back to the night she met Fabio at the club. She thought of all the blood shed over the years. She knew what she had to do and was ready for whatever comes next. Jamila walked to her phone and called Deniro. After two rings he the phone picked up.

"Hello, can I speak to Mr. Deniro?"

"Who is speaking?"

"Let him know it's Red Invee."

The phone went silent for a minute.

"Hello Red Invee, how are you?"

"Still alive. We need to talk face to face."

"And why would I want to do that?"

"Because it will look bad hiding in a house somewhere. Now what would your men think who been dying in the streets and you hiding when we could have ended this war."

"Red Invee, you know nothing will give me more pleasure than to watch you fucking die."

"Likewise."

"I'll meet with you Red Invee and where would you like to have this meeting at?"

"How about you and I have lunch tomorrow at the Fox Inn in Harlem?"

"Sounds good to me."

"What time Mr. Deniro?"

"2 p.m."

"I'll see you then," hanging up the phone.

Frankie was at the door to her office, and he heard every word Jamila said. He turned around and walked off before she could see him. Picking up the phone she called Lorenzo as she took a seat at her desk. He picked the phone up on the first ring.

"What's up Jamila?"

"Look this is everything I need you to do ASAP."

"I'm listening."

"I need ten kilos and make sure you take our tag off of them. The three guns used to kill Mayor Oakland and the same bomb that was used to take the FBI building down. I need all of this today and bring it to me. You, Young Boy and Badii, I need ya tomorrow. We have a meeting to go to by 2 p.m."

"Ok, I'll go take care of all of this now."

Hanging up the phone with Lorenzo she called Crystal.

"Hello this is Crystal."

"Hey, this is Jamila."

"Oh my God are you ok? Hold on one second." Crystal walked outside the building to the back alley so no one could here he talk.

"Ok, I can talk now."

"Yea, I am." replied Jamila.

"The FBI reopened your case but it's in a secret place and me nor Jatavious know where. They have you on the top of the list as The Black Queen Don."

"Crystal, I need your help."

"Jamila, I don't know what I can do for you. This is way out of my hands. FBI agents and two DEA agents killed in a yearlong investigation."

"Crystal, how long have you been trying to get Mr. Deniro?"

"For over five years now."

"If I help you get him can you get me off and have my name cleared?" asked Jamila.

"Help me get him? What you mean?"

"I can prove he had Mayor Oakland killed and did the bombing that killed the agents."

"If you can prove that I know I can have a talk with my boss and I might be able to help."

"Well, you have till tomorrow by 11 am to let me know."

"Jamila to make this work we need to get him red handed."

"What if ya pull him over and everything I said is in the trunk of his car?"

"Let me call you back and see what I can do."

"Can I call you back on this number?"

"Yea, you can what time?"

"Give me three hours at the most.?

"I'll be waiting on your call."

Jamila hung up the phone. After hanging up with Crystal, Jamila made one last call to Anthony. After two rings he picked up.

"Hi Anthony, how you been?"

"Good and you Ms. LaCross?"

"I'm good. I'm calling you because I need a big favor."

"What's that and how can I help you?"

"I have two duffle bags that I need you to put in somebody car for me, without being seen."

"Yea, I can do that for you."

"Anthony, it's not just anybody's car. It's Mr. Deniro from the Deniro family."

"Whoa, that's an all-new ball game. How am I supposed to get close to the man's car?" asked Anthony.

"I have a meeting with him tomorrow at the Fox Inn. You can do it then."

"Ms. LaCross, I will never tell you no, but you are asking a lot. If you don't mind me asking, What's in the bag? Is it important?"

"I have 30,000 for you to get it done."

"Ok, bet."

"Thank you, Anthony."

"No problem. I'll be up there waiting for you."

"I'll have Lorenzo give you the bags."

"I'll be waiting on him. I'll see you tomorrow Anthony."

*****

Frankie walked off from Jamila's office door before she saw him. Making his way back to his limo where Fabio was waiting on him at.

"Fabio, we need to talk."

"About what?"

"Get in and I'll tell you on the way back to the meat market."

Once in the limo Frankie pulled a cigar out and lit it. "I just heard Jamila and Deniro talking over the phone. She has plans on meeting him tomorrow at the Fox Inn in Harlem."

"She told us that a few days ago."

"No, Fabio it was more to the conversation. It's something I can't put my finger on. I just have a funny feeling about it all."

"So, what are you saying Frankie?"

"I don't trust nothing right now until all of this is over."

"Frankie do you hear yourself? She had Ms. Simpson killed because what she did to you. Put you in a big house, took care of all your business while you were in the hospital. Got your cocaine back and took care of the case against us and you say you don't trust her? Frankie you are tripping."

"Fabio just trust me right now. I have always been with you and I always sided with you. So now I'm asking you to side with me. Just give me a few days and we will go back and check on her."

"This is wrong Frankie but I'm with you." Blowing smoke out his mouth Frankie ain't say nothing else for the rest of the ride.

*****

Jamila had a wine glass full of Ace of Spade taking sips as she thought back of some of the things her father always told her. She had a flash back of a conversation she had sitting on his lap when she was only nine years old.

"Dad, can I ask you a question without you getting mad?"

"Sure, sweet pea what is it?"

"Do you lie at your job?"

"Sweet pea listen to me, in my line of work I have to use selective honesty and generosity because it helps me disarm my enemies. Remember the goal is to always win. Conceal your intentions and your enemy will always be off balance and in the dark."

"Why do we have enemy's dad? Who would want to hurt us?"

"You will always have enemy's no matter what you do sweet pea. I want you to promise me something."

"Sure dad."

"Promise me that if the day ever come, that you will do what you have to do to crush your enemies totally."

Looking up at her dad. "I promise dad."

"Let's pinky promise."

"I pinky promise dad. Dad you will always be with me forever."

Taking a deep breathe he looked at her. "If you ever need me and I'm not here, just think back about what we always talk about sweet pea."

Jamila's thoughts were interrupted by the ringing of her phone.

"Hello Crystal?"

"Yes, Jamila,"

"Listen if you can get us everything you said tomorrow on Deniro, you are off the case load."

"Ok, be ready for me to call you around 3:30 pm tomorrow in Harlem by Park. When I call, I'll have the car and plate number for you. I'll call thirty minutes before they leave so be ready."

"Ok, we are going to be on standby for tomorrow."

*****

Checking her gun after taking a deep breath, Jamila pulled in the parking lot of the Fox Inn. It was 1:45pm she had Lorenzo and Badii watching her back from another car and Young Boy inside at a table just in case things went wrong.

Deniro had someone watching her when she pulled up. Ten minutes later Deniro pulled up him and three of his guys got out the car and walked into the Fox Inn.

Jamila stood up when she saw him coming her way.

"Mr. Deniro?"

"Mrs. LaCross."

He gave her a light hug and a kiss on the cheek.

"Shall we sit Mr. Deniro?" said Jamila.

"Sure, Red Invee I see you are by yourself."

"I told you I just wanted to talk."

"So how you been Red Invee?"

"Like I told you before I'm still alive. Let's quit the small talk Mr. Deniro, you came by my restaurant and talked with Lorenzo and told him you have no problems with me or my family. Then you set up a hit on me. I'm a little confused."

"War is war Red Invee. How I know what your plans was for me? You never reached back out to me at all. Being the head of your family I'm sure you understand, I had to look out for my family and protect them no matter what."

"I do understand that Mr. Deniro I have no problems with your family, but I will go to war if that's what it takes to get your respect."

"I do respect you and your family, and I might have been wrong for spilling the first blood. I was protecting my family and I will not take that back. With that being said I do not have no problems with you Red Invee, but I do know how close you and Frankie are. So, do I have to worry about that?"

"No, you don't."

"Well, then we have nothing else to talk about Ms. LaCross."

"Mr. Deniro you are right and thank you for taking the time out to talk to me."

"Thank you for the call, Ms. LaCross."

With a light hug Deniro walked off. Jamila overheard him say, "fuck that nigga. She will be dead just like Frankie will be." She smiled and picked up her phone and called Crystal.

"Hello."

"Hey, he's leaving in a dark blue Lexus. It's three of them in the car."

"So, what now Boss?"

"We will kill Frankie once he is dead, we will go after Red Invee. This meeting just gave us something to take care of Frankie without the LaCross family getting involved."

As Mr. Deniro's car pulled out the Fox Inn they were surrounded by ten FBI agents with guns drawn out on them. Crystal got out the car while Mr. Deniro and his men were hand cuffed on the ground.

"What the fuck is the meaning of all of this?"

"Mr. Deniro, we have a warrant to search your house and car. Pop open his trunk and let's see what we can find."

When they popped the trunk, there was two duffle bags in there filled with cocaine, guns and two bombs like the ones that were used on the building that blew up and killed the six agents.

"Sir, you might want to take a look at this."

"Crystal, you busted his ass."

"Mr. Deniro, you might want to call that high-priced attorney you have because you're going to need him. Get them out of here."

"Crystal, I don't know who your source was, but this was a big bust today. You should be proud of yourself."

*****

Jamila met Lorenzo twenty minutes later at the pond.

"So how was the meeting?"

"All lies and fake smiles, but it is over that's all that matters. I see everything was good with the bags going into Mr. Deniro's trunk."

"While you were on the inside, we had a problem, but I took care of it, come check it out. We had someone trying to take that gift out of the car."

"Who?" Jamila asked.

Lorenzo popped the trunk and one of Deniro's men was laying there dead.

"When I saw him going by the trunk of the car, I pulled up on him and asked did he need some help and took him out."

"You know what," said Jamila, "I don't care what you do with his body. Dump his body off somewhere. I ended the war."

"What you think they going to do with Deniro?"

"Only time will tell. I'm about to go lay down for a little while."

"I'll be out here when you wake up," Lorenzo said closing the trunk of the car.

*****

Frankie was watching the newscast as they were talking about the bust of Deniro, and how there was two bombs in the trunk of the car that was identified as the same ones that was used to bomb the building the four FBI agents and two DEA agents were killed. Where his case and two more was being held in and how the guns were linked to the same ones used to kill Mayor Oakland and the two police officer four years ago. There was a large amount of cocaine in the trunk as well. She wasn't trying to betray me. She was setting him up to take the fall all along Frankie said to himself. Fabio walked in the back room at the meat market.

"I'm guessing you are seeing the news I was just watching it. So, what you going to say to her now?"

"There's nothing we can say to her. What is done is done."

"Frankie, she knew we left her when it was crunch time. Anybody can see that the day at the cemetery when she said she was going to meet Deniro. We distance ourselves. Now look all along she had a plan and it worked. She planted everything on him and cleared our name. I just wanted to tell you that. I'm going back up front now. Just remember I sided with you."

When Fabio walked out Frankie picked up the phone and called Jamila, but she didn't answer. He knew what Fabio was saying was right he fucked up and might have lost her trust now.

*****

"Deniro, attorney visit," the county jail guard yelled.

Walking into the attorney booth, Deniro sat down and was looking through the glass window at his attorney Michael Kent. As he picked up the phone, "Mr. Deniro, how are you holding up in here?"

"Like hell in this fucking shit hole."

"I'm not going to lie to you it doesn't look good at all. They did a ballistics test on the guns and they are the same weapons that were used to kill Mayor Oakland and the police officers four years ago. The two bombs are the same ones that were used to bomb the FBI headquarters not even three months ago and I'm not even worried about the cocaine, that's the least of your problems."

"I was set the fuck up, ain't none of that mine. I don't even know how it got in my trunk. What the DA talking about?" asked Mr. Deniro.

"I'm not going to lie to you, he's asking for the death sentence. He got the weapons that were used to kill the Mayor of NYC and two NYPD officers. And he has the same homemade bombs that was used to kill four FBI agents and two DEA agents. That's nine upstanding citizens that worked for the government dead. We are not going to win this trial. We can pick twelve jurors from anywhere and they still going to find you guilty because #1 you are a Mafia member #2 your criminal record and #3 your car had two duffle bags in it with guns, drugs and bomb. The DA is going to say you was trying to get rid of it somewhere. You know how the game goes.

In the court room it's about who can tell the better story for the people to believe."

"Fuck, so what's the plea?" said Deniro.

"Three life sentences plus a hundred and twenty years and you have to give up all your sources. He will recommend you go to a private prison where you can live out the rest of your days."

"So, I have to become a fucking rat?"

"If you want to live."

"How long I got to think about this?"

"One week. I'll be back Wednesday to see you.

Hanging up the phone Deniro watched as his attorney walked out the booth.

SAYNOMORE

Chapter Fourteen

Pulling up at the Red Carpet, Frankie and Fabio stepped out the limo. They were going to see Vinnie Lenacci.

"Fabio, did Vinnie ever say what he wanted to talk about?"

"No, he just asked could we come and see him. That's all he asked. I told him we will be by there tomorrow by noon."

Walking inside Vinnie was at the back table in VIP talking on the phone when they walked up.

"Hey, let me call you back, I have some guests that just walked in."

"Frankie good to see you."

"You too, Vinnie."

Getting up shaking Frankie and Fabio's hand. "Please both of you have a seat. Do you want something to drink?"

"No, we are fine."

"Ok then. Frankie let's talk, the Lenacci and Landon families have been friends for over twenty years and we always had a very strong relationship. And the Lenacci family respects that family. Then we hear you take a black female under your wing and out of nowhere she starts running her own Mafia family called the LaCross family using your last name Fabio. What's so crazy it's a black female Don running Queens. Now me and Red Invee had two or three sit downs and talked. She opened doors to me on something she is very smart and wise. When she went to war with my family, I just knew she was a dead female, but she came out on top. When Deniro came to talk to me with Marcus I told them both they are dead men walking. And that they had one shot with her. They both looked at me in the eyes and laughed. Now one of them is dead and the other one is looking at life in prison. But the reason I called you here is because Red Invee listens to you. It's no secret Frankie Red Invee is becoming too strong. She is doing what Tony did in only a few years with the Judges, Da and cops. She could have killed me a few years back, but she came and talked to me and told me don't nobody else has to die, but one man. And with them words our war was over. I respect her and how she runs Queens, but I also have contacts in Queens that I use to do business with that I can't no more because she won't allow it."

"So, I'm asking you can you talk with her about me opening up a car shop out there to maintain a strong friendship with my contact because Red Invee will not open that door for me. So, I was hoping you may be able to open that door for me by talking to her."

"Vinnie you are right on two things one we have been friends for a very long time and two Red Invee is becoming very powerful, and I don't think she knew that. She has a very strong mind and when it's made up it's made up. The reason Deniro family as well as your family lost to her is because Tony, Sammy, Sunnie, Alex and Deniro all under-estimated her because she was black and yes, I did show her the ropes but that was it, everything else she did on her own."

"My question to you Frankie is, can you talk with her about letting me open up my shop on her turf with her blessings?"

"I would but now me and Red Invee are having our ups and downs at this moment as we speak."

"I hope not to be going to your funeral next Frankie."

They both started laughing.

"No Vinnie, me and her will never cross that line."

"Fabio, you haven't said a word since you been here."

"I was showing respect to you two and listening to y'all conversation. Mr. Lenacci, Red Invee is a cold-hearted killer, and she don't second guess at all when it comes down to pulling the trigger. I brought her into this life. I gave her the money and business to start up with. I was there when she killed Bull and shot Sammy in the face. One thing she ain't going to do is let anyone bully her. She will die first. She already put a gun to my face and told me she will kill me."

"So, let me get this right, the female you helped put a gun to your face?" said Vinnie. "If it was me, she would be dead already."

"If history recalls that same female killed four very powerful men in your family already. Mr. Lenacci the best thing I can tell you is whatever positive grounds you and Red Invee are on, it will be smart to keep it that way," replied Fabio.

"So are ya still allies Frankie?"

"Yes, we are Vinnie. I look at her as my daughter.

"I respect that Frankie. Well thank both of y'all for stopping by and I will take your advice Fabio. Y'all have a good day."

"You too, Vinnie."

SAYNOMORE

Chapter Fifteen

"DA Moore, how's it going?"

"Mr. Stone, it's funny running into you in the courthouse."

"Yea, I'm here to check on a new bill."

"Well, if you ain't busy, how about you have a bite to eat with me in the food court?"

"That sounds good to me. So, what you been up to Moore?"

"Just working this case day and night."

"What case?" asked Jatavious with a puzzled look on his face.

"The Deniro case. We got him red-handed, guns, drugs, bombs. I was asking for the death sentence, but me and his attorney been talking. He decided to cooperate and give up his sources. This might be the crackdown we needed if what his attorney is saying is true. We are about to have a major blow in NYC. I'm talking about drug contacts, hints on who's the new Don since Tony got killed. Crooked cops, DA's, Judge's he's spilling the beans on everything."

"That's great news Moore. We needed some help cleaning the street's up. It's about time we get rid of the garbage. So, when you plan on seeing him?" asked Jatavious.

"Within the next two weeks."

"Hello, I am so sorry for the wait. What can I get you two to eat?"

"I'll have a burger and fries. What about you, Moore?"

"Same thing."

*****

Frankie was riding in his limo through the city talking with Fabio when his phone went off.

"Hello, it's Jatavious we need to talk ASAP. So, stop whatever you are doing and meet me in Harlem behind Pandoras Box. I'll be there in 30 minutes Frankie."

"I'm on my way now."

Frankie hung up the phone and looked at Fabio.

"Who was that?"

"Jatavious, he just told me to meet him in Harlem. Mitch, change of plans take us to Harlem to Pandoras Box."

"What's going on Frankie?"

"I don't know. He just told me to stop what I was doing and meet him in Harlem. So, it must be important."

"You think it might be another case against us?"

"No, it was a worry in his voice. It's something else. We will find out in a few minutes."

When they pulled up Frankie and Fabio got out and walked to the back door.

"Fabio, knock two times and when the slide opens say Forest Bones."

Fabio knocked two times and the voice from the other side said, "Who is it?"

"Forest Bones."

When the door opened a 7-foot guard was standing there. "Last door on the right, he's waiting on you now." Walking through the door Frankie saw Jatavious looking out the window smoking a cigar.

Without looking back, "We have a problem Frankie, a big one.

"And what is that?"

"Deniro is cooperating with the DA. He agreed to give up all of his sources, Judges, DA's, Cops." Standing there listening to every word Jatavious said Frankie looked at Fabio and closed his eyes and shook his head.

"Frankie, I don't think I have to say what needs to be done."

"How long do we have?"

"Two weeks but I'm only giving you seven days. You, Red Invee and everyone else. This is going to effect. This is bigger than John Gotti and Sammy the Bull."

"He's locked up, how am I supposed to get to him?"

"My job is to keep the police off your ass, and I don't ask questions how, so that's not my problem, just get it done. Because my name doesn't need to come up and I'm sure you don't need him talking about certain things, like some bodies that don't need to be found. I have to get back to my office. Seven days Frankie, Fabio you have a good afternoon." Jatavious walked out the door.

"What now Frankie?" asked Fabio

"We kill Deniro. Come on let's go I have some calls to make."

*****

"Ms. LaCross you have a phone call on line one."

"Thank you, Jasmine."

Picking up her office phone walking in her bird cage, "Ms. LaCross speaking."

"Hello Jamila, it's Morwell."

"Hey, why are you calling me on this phone?"

"Because your other phone might be tapped. I need you to come sees me, it's very important."

"I'll catch a flight tomorrow morning and come down."

"Jamila, I don't think you understand, I need you to leave now," replied Morwell.

"Ok, I'm on my way. I'll see you in a few hours."

"I'll be waiting on you."

Hanging up the phone Jamila talking to herself as she calls Lorenzo. "What could be so wrong with Morwell that he needs me to leave right now?"

"Hello Lorenzo listen, I'm leaving to go see Morwell right now. I need you to come close up for me tonight."

"Is everything ok?" asked Lorenzo "With Morwell?"

"I don't know, I will talk with you when I get back. I have to go."

"Be safe."

"Trust me, I will."

*****

Oso walked through the doors. "Morwell you wanted to see me?"

"Yea have someone pick Red Invee up at the airport. She's on her way down here now. Her plane should be landing in the next few hours."

"I'm on it now."

"Make sure you bring her right back here Oso. This is very important and put a private plane on standby for her to get back tonight."

"I got this bro, trust me."

"I do trust you, that's why I depend on you so much."

Oso nodded his head and walked out the door. "Morwell do you think you can trust her to get it done?"

"If Deniro talk a lot of people are going to go down and we need them where they are. This can be a domino effect. Stone said he was going to take care of it but, every plan A needs a plan B. And I'm not going to gamble this empire on one man's word."

"So, what make you gamble on Red Invee?"

"Because I told Stone that Mayor Oakland was in my way and she killed him within three days, that's why I trust her. Come on, I have to go to the farm."

*****

Walking in the den room, Frankie looked around at the round table and saw everyone there he called.

"I called you all here tonight because by now I'm sure everyone here knows that Deniro has broken the code of silence. He decided to cooperate with the DA for a life sentence, He's a fucking rat that needs to be killed. We are talking over twenty years of hits, murders, assassinations, secrets, drugs, Transactions. Judges, DA's, cops that work for us. Gambling rings, underground fights etc."

"Frankie, do we even know where he is being held at?"

"Scott, no I don't. When I heard he became a snitch, I ain't want to believe it."

"So how we suppose to kill a man that we don't even know where they hiding him at?"

"Mr. Gambino, I'm thinking we kidnap his wife, son, daughter. Let it be known and let him kill himself."

"And if he doesn't Frankie we are fucked."

"It's five powerful families at this table, Landon, Scott, Gambino, Lenacci and Deniro. I hate to say this but the Deniro family, this really falls on."

"Vinnie, we understand he is a rat and we going to do what we need to do."

"Frankie, how long do we have?"

"From what I was told DA Moore is going to have a meeting with him in fourteen days. But we have a window of seven days that start tonight."

"What about Red Invee from what I'm told she got a few Judge's in her pocket. She can't find out where he is at Frankie?"

"I don't know, I called her here too, but I was told she is out the states right now as of a few hours ago."

"Does she know about this?"

"I don't know Vinnie."

"Bottom line, if he's going to give up that kind of information that can bring the NYC crime families down, meaning us. He's going to be well guarded and I'm pretty sure, so is his family Vinnie. It's five families here and this is what it is. There's a hit on Deniro and his head is our prize. Let's call our sources and get it done cause if not we all are going to have cases. Everyone agree?"

Frankie looked at everyone as they raised, they hand.

*****

"Jamila, it's good to see you thank you for coming down."

"It's good to see you to Morwell. What was so important that I had to come down here tonight?"

"Jamila come walk with me. I want to introduce you to somebody, a business partner of mine. You know why I made it so far in this life?" said Morwell. "Because when I was fifteen years old, I learned people only respect violence and sometimes getting your hands dirty is the only way to make somethings right. A weak heart will get you killed, and a friend will betray your trust. But a business partner is loyal because of the investment he or she put in."

Walking to the bottom of the hill Jamila saw four guys on the knees with the hands tied behind their backs. A man was talking to some of the guards with guns in their hands.

"Carlos, come here please. I'd like to introduce you to Jamila LaCross."

Jamila was looking at the heavy-set bald head man walking her way with a white suit on. "It's nice to meet you Jamila, I heard so much about you."

"It's nice to meet you Carlos."

Jamila looked back at the guys on the knees and back at Carlos.

"Jamila, I have more cocaine than anyone, but you see these four guys over here? One of them messed up five bricks of my cocaine. I have no time in my line of business for fuck up's."

Listening to his heavy Dominican accent and looking at all the guys walking around with AR15's. Morwell walked up to each of the guys on their knees and put the gun to the back of their heads and blew they brains out. He handed the gun back to his bodyguard.

"Now that that is taken care of let's go talk Jamila about the reason, I called you down here tonight. There's a problem in New York City that needs to be dealt with right away that will affect my business and you Jamila. I got a call today telling me Deniro has become an informant. If he tells on the right people, we can lose hundreds of millions of dollars. I have friends that can't let that happen too. Come inside Jamila, please take a seat. So, do you understand the problem we are having?"

"I do, but I don't even know where they are keeping him."

"A good friend of mine told me he is being held in a private jail. But he also told me they will be transporting him next week closer to Brooklyn for his meeting with DA Moore. That is the only window I can give you Jamila."

"Can you get me the name of one of the guards that will be transporting him?" asked Jamila.

"Let me work on that."

"So, I can trust you to handle this situation?"

"How many days do I have?"

"Seven at the most."

"As long as you get me the name, I'll take care of the rest from there."

"Good, that's all I need to hear. Now Oso has a car and plane on standby for you."

"I'll be in touch Morwell and Carlos, it was nice meeting you."

*****

Walking in the pool hall stopping at the door Detective Boatman looked around when Tony Pain walked up to him. "You lost?"

Taking off his glasses placing them in his top right pocket then looking at Tony Pain.

"Look here, I'm the real fucking bad guy so I ain't never lost. Now be a good door boy and let cap know that Detective Boatman is here now hop hop. Walking to the bar, ah let me get a blue motherfucker," as he sat down and turned his back to the bar.

"Here you go that's $8," turning around on the stool.

"Here you go $20 keep the change."

"Detective Boatman glad to see you dropped by."

"We have something to talk about cap."

"Come to the back let's talk detective close that door behind you."

Closing the door behind him Detective Boatman took a seat in front of the desk.

"How you been Boatman?"

"It's Detective Boatman and I'm fine. Let me get to the point why I'm here. Deniro had me take care of Mickey and a few days later he gets his self-locked up looking at the death sentence. But here's my problem, I ain't get paid and that's bad business like two dicks with no bitch. So, I'm here to collect $30,000."

"I remember something like that Deniro was telling me. That was that body floating in the Hudson River two weeks ago. Ah Pain come here go get $30 large from the back room and bring it back to me."

Pulling out a pack of cigarettes, "have one detective?"

"I'll pass, I hear Deniro is about to do a lot of talking."

"Yea I heard that too."

"You ain't worried?"

"He might talk on what you did for the family."

"Not at all, he will be dead before he gets one word out."

"And how you know that?"

Just then Tony Pain walked back in the room with the money in an envelope.

"Give it to the Detective."

Checking the money placing it in his pocket.

"Do you know where they are keeping him at?"

"I have no clue."

"So, how do you know he will be dead and can't tell on you too?"

"Because ya going to kill him. See I ain't worried because the spark he has on me ain't shit to the wildfire he has on ya."

"Take care cap, here's my card if you need me." He passed him his card as he walked out the door.

Chapter Sixteen

Jamila woke up at 7:30 that morning with a text in her phone from Morwell.

Derrick Mosley

214 Zion Street

Deer Park, New York

She replied back, "copy."

Getting dressed and meeting her driver outside. "Good morning Ms. LaCross", as he opened the door for her.

"Good Morning Steve. There's a change of plans this morning. Here, I wrote down this address. This is where I need you to take me this morning."

"Yes Ms. LaCross."

"Pull up on the street but not in front of the house."

Jamila looked to see her phone was ringing.

"Hello?"

"Hey, I was just checking on you. How did the meeting go with Morwell?"

"Lorenzo, that's a long story. I just got in at 1 this morning and I'm about to take care of something right now for him about what we talked about. Can you open up for me today this morning?"

"Sure, I got it."

"Thanks Lorenzo," I see you in a little while.

"Ms. LaCross we are pulling up on the block now. There's a blue car pulling out the driveway with a man in it."

"Follow that car Steve. See if you can get his plate numbers when he stops. He's pulling up at the Starbucks now."

"Pull over in the parking lot with him, but not to close."

Jamila watched as he got out the car. He was light skin 5'9" with deep waves. He was skinny and didn't look to be no more than thirty-one years old. She also noticed his wedding ring as he walked in the Starbucks.

"What now Ms. LaCross?"

"I want to see where he goes when he leaves from here. Hold on to that address because when you drop me off, I want you to go take pictures of everyone who lives in that house. Kids and wife and tomorrow is when I'll meet up with him and have a sit down with him."

"He's leaving now get ready to follow him."

"I think he works for the SWAT team because of the sticker he has on his windshield."

"It doesn't make me no never mind who he works for, go ahead and start following him."

"After twenty minutes he pulled in at the 25th precinct."

"You can drop me off at the restaurant and go take care of what I asked you to do Steve."

"Yes, Ms. LaCross."

Pulling up at Jelani's, Steve opened the door for her.

"Go handle that Steve and I'll see you tomorrow morning."

"I'll go do that now."

Walking inside she met Lorenzo at the front desk.

"Hey, you took care of that this morning?"

"Yea, I did, let's go talk."

"We can talk in your office."

"So, what was so important that you had to leave and go down to Dominican Republic last night?"

"Deniro is talking. He's making a deal with the DA and Morwell needs him dead before he gets the chance to talk. His meeting is in two weeks, but next week he's going to be on a bus coming closer for this meeting. Right now, he's at a private jail. I followed one of the officers who will be transporting him. The only thing I can think of is we have to hit him on the bus. It might be four guards on there at the most. If he talks that can fuck us all up."

"You know what Jamila, yesterday after you left Frankie called here looking for you. He said there was a meeting with the 7 and they needed you there. I'm willing to bet that was what it was about. So how would we hit him on the bus? We don't even know what time they will be transporting him."

"I'll have all that information tomorrow. But I'll need you, Badii and Young Boy even Muscle to be on standby when I do call. To let you know the time and place. I don't care if we have to kill everyone on the bus to get to him but, this week Deniro must die no questions asked."

*****

Fabio walked in the meeting at the meat Market Frankie was having with Vinnie.

"Excuse me, how you are doing Vinnie?"

"I'm good Fabio."

"Frankie you were right his family is well guarded. There were two cars outside his house. There's no getting to his wife or kids at all. When the kids went to school, they had a police escort. One car took the kids and the other stayed at the house with the wife. We been watching them since the meeting yesterday."

"So, what now?"

"What you think Vinnie?"

"I don't know Frankie this is a tough one. This ain't going to be a walk in the park. He's well-guarded and so is his family. We might have to swallow the pill and get ready for this domino affect that's about to hit us all Frankie. What about his attorney?"

"Frankie you think he might know where he is being held at? Because he has the right to see his attorney."

"No Vinnie from what I'm told his attorney can't see him until the day of the meeting because it's a security breach."

"Do we even know what Judge is going to try his case?"

"No, it's a federal judge and his name is unknown right now. Let me make a few phone calls and I'll let you know something tomorrow."

*****

"Good morning Ms. LaCross."

"Good morning Steve. Did you take care of what I asked you do?"

"Yes, here you go."

Jamila was looking at the pictures as he talked. He has two kids a boy and a girl named Innocence and Kenny. They both go to a daycare called Kids Stay and play off of 110. His wife works at JCPenney," replied Steve.

"Good take me to Starbucks. We will wait for him there." Jamila watched as he walked in. "I'll be out in a few minutes, Steve. Keep the car running."

As Jamila walked in, she walked behind Derrick as he was placing his order.

"Hello, may I take your order?"

"I'll have the same thing he is having. That cup of coffee sounds good."

"Ok, that will be $2.50."

"Here you go."

"Thank you and here is your change."

"Excuse me sir, if you ain't too busy can I have a word with you?"

Derrick looked at Jamila's long curly black hair with her hazel eyes and caramel skin. And he noticed how her dress was hugging her hourglass body down to her open toe shoes.

"Sure, I have a minute. Come let's have a seat and talk. I've never seen you here before and I come here every morning."

"It's my first time, but I really need to talk with you about something very important Derrick."

"How you know my name?"

"Let's just say it's my job to know the people I need to know."

Jamila looked dead in his eyes when she said that. Derrick pulled his badge out and placed it on the table.

"Make sure your conversation is clean."

"I'm not worried about your badge, I have a few of them myself who work for me."

At that time the waiter brought them their cups of coffee. "Here you go enjoy!"

"First off, let me introduce myself. My name is Jamila LaCross or Red Invee, it doesn't matter what you call me." Derrick looked at her and knew who she was. There had been briefings about her.

Before he never seen her picture. He just knew the stories and the name Red Invee.

"In life Derrick you have choices, just like the red and blue pill. You can except the truth, or you can deny the truth. It's all up to you in that split moment. I'm giving you a choice today. You can leave this Starbucks $300,000 richer, or you can leave this Starbucks thinking I'm a joke and gambling with the lives of your loved ones. And you only have until this conversation is over to make your choice. I know you are a transport officer for Mr. Deniro. You will tell me when he is leaving and also how many officers are with him, including the time and place down to the tee. You will not skip a beat on this. Do you understand me?"

"Now hear my words, I will not hurt no officers, All I want is Deniro."

"And if I say no?" said Derrick.

Jamila took a sip of her coffee and reached in her purse pulling out the pictures of his wife and kids.

"You have a beautiful family, is that the gamble you want to take the blue pill?" Looking at his wife and kids he knew this wasn't a gamble he wanted to take.

"I know your wife Shelly works at JCPenney and both your kids go to the Daycare Kids stay and play off of 110. I'm not here to threaten your family my first offer was $300,000. Now do we have a deal?"

"And I have your word no harm will come to my family?" asked Derrick.

"You have my word Innocence, Kenny as well as Shelby, no harm will come to them. And your money will be up front. You also have my word if you fuck me, I will kill you and your family in the worst way. And make you watch and kill you in the fucking end of it all very slowly."

"They are moving him two days from now. We're taking Riverside Drive to Kentwood Drive. It's four of us detailing."

"What time are ya moving him?" replied Jamila.

"Between 8 am and 1 pm."

"Here is my number if anything changes, and like I said I'm paying you upfront." Reaching in her purse she pulled out her cellphone and called Steve.

"Hello, Mrs. LaCross," he answered.

"You can put my money on his car." She disconnected the call without uttering another word.

"Derrick I could make you a millionaire over time, remember the red or blue pill the choice is yours. And this was a good cup of coffee. Thank you I have to get it again." She turned swiftly, leaving Derrick at the table as she walked out of Starbucks to where Steve was waiting on her.

"Everything good, Ms. LaCross?"

"Everything went perfect Steve, take me to the restaurant."

*****

"Frankie, honestly, I'm disappointed about this phone call. I thought I could put my trust in you."

"You asked me to clean a mess up with a man who is in witness protection. And you don't you even know where's he's at? His family is well guarded. Give me something to work with to get this done."

Jatavious walked to his office window and looked out it.

"Frankie, I told you before I don't ask you how to do my job, so you don't ask me how to do your job. The only thing I can tell you is that he will be talking to DA Moore in a few days. Now please don't call me back until this problem is taken care of."

With them words Jatavious hung up the phone. Frankie placed the phone down on his desk and placed his hands over his face and take two deep breaths. Knowing he had to have someone pay DA Moore a visit. This could fuck things up or make them better but what choice did he have with only four days left before the meeting with DA Moore and Deniro. The clock was ticking, and he was running out of time. Picking up his phone he called Fabio. He knew what he had to do. It was a chance he had to take.

*****

Lorenzo, Badii, Young Boy and Muscle was in the office waiting on Jamila to show up.

"This must be big."

"It is Young Boy, Jamila had to go to the Dominican Republic behind this one."

"What's it about Lorenzo?"

"She's going to let you know when she comes in Badii. It's best you hear it from her. She knows all the details front and back. In situations like this somebody got to die. That's why we are here just like with Mayor Oakland. We just got to get our hands dirty."

Jamila walked in the back door where nobody saw her come in.

"You're right, Muscle, somebody has to die within the next forty-eight hours, and we can't have any slipups. It's going to be your four and I'll be watching making sure everything goes right. It's going to be two cars, and everyone is going to be dressed in all black with AR15's. We are going to cut the bus off from the front and back. You see these two blocks of C4, Badii and Lorenzo you will show them the bus driver and tell him to open the door. Young Boy and Muscle will go on the bus and shot Deniro point blank in the head three times. You will not touch any guards. Once Deniro is dead we leave. Does everyone understand?"

"What time is all of this going down?"

"Between 8am and 1pm. I'll be watching for the bus, so, Lorenzo, make sure you watch out for my call. Everyone be on standby because when I call, that means it's time."

*****

Deniro was laying in his bed sleep when he heard a knock at the door. Deniro woke up. "You're getting transported within the next two hours," the CO told him.

Getting himself together he knew he was going to meet DA Moore to make his deal. He didn't know how all of that got in his trunk of his car. But he knew somebody set him up and if he was going to take the fall, everyone around him was going to take the fall with him. He was not going down alone in his mind the whole ship was about to sink with him, his mind was made up.

Opening the door, he looked at the two officers with cuffs and shackles.

"You ready to take this ride?"

"You are acting like I'm about to go to Six Flags."

"Deniro let's cuff up," turning around lifting his leg up one by one as they shackled his ankles.

"How long is the ride?"

"Don't worry about it when you get there, you get there."

Taking step by step getting on the bus as they were placing him in his seat.

"All right boys, let's rock and roll."

Jamila got a text that said, "We are moving now." She was already waiting, and everyone was in place. She saw the bus coming down the street and called Lorenzo. "Be ready in three minutes."

"How long before we get there?" said Deniro, "it feels like I been on this bus forever."

"Don't worry hold your horses Deniro. You'll be able to tell on everyone in a few more minutes."

"What the fuck?" the driver said as the bus came to a fast stop being cut off by two cars in the front and in the rear of the bus. Lorenzo jumped out with the AR15 pointed at the window as Badii placed the two blocks of C4 on the side of the bus.

"Open the door or everyone dies on this bitch." Young Boy and Muscle walked up behind the bus pointing their guns at the window.

"Open the door, I'm not dying over this scum." replied Derrick.

Lorenzo put up five fingers and started counting down from five. Just then the doors opened. Deniro looked at them as they walked on the bus.

"Everyone to the back now. Hands where I can see them. Put them in the air," said Muscle. Lorenzo and Badii watched as Muscle and Young Boy was on the bus walking up to Deniro.

"I guess this is my jail break."

"No, you are a fucking rat. This is your death sentence," Muscle said as he pointed his gun at his head pulling the trigger three times blowing his brains out. Deniro's body hit the side of the seat as he kept opening fire on him.

"Come on let's go."

They ran off the bus to their cars and peeled off. Jamila saw everything from the top of the building she was on when they pulled off. She walked away. It was all done in four minutes. She flipped a coin in the air and said, "job done."

*****

"What the fuck happened out here? How the fuck did they know when he was being transported? I want some damn answers now."

"Chief Tadem, we don't know. From what the jail guards said they blocked them off and put C4 on the side of the bus. They thought it was a jail break. But once on the bus they killed him and left."

"Get these news teams back and make sure I get a full report on everything on my desk." Chief Tadem looked as they took Deniro's body off the bus in a black bag.

"Frankie you are seeing this?"

"Yea Fabio someone took care of Deniro. They said he got shot six times in the chest and three times in the head. Two cars blocked them off and put C4 on the bus walked up to him and killed him, then left."

Smoking his cigar and watching the news as they took Deniro body off the bus all Frankie could ask himself was, "Who killed him and how they knew when he would be transported?" The main question who assassinated Deniro the news was asking.

*****

"I can't believe this shit, you are telling me four men stopped the bus walked on it and killed Deniro," walking back and forth in his office. "He was the key, the weak link, we been looking for. We had him and hours before he can cooperate with us, he gets killed. What a fucking morning I'm having. I'm on my way down there now." Hanging up the phone DA Moore picked up his coat from the back of his chair and walked out his office slamming the door behind him.

*****

Sitting with his legs crossed smoking his Cuban cigar blowing smoke out his mouth as he watched the news. Morwell got up and fixed his tie.

"So, what was you saying Carlos?"

"Can I put my trust in her? I think the answer is being talked about right now on the news."

"I was wrong she took care of the business one time asked."

"That's why I put my trust in her, let me call her now."

*****

"Closing the warehouse doors Lorenzo walked up on Badii and Young Boy.

"Burn the cars Muscle. Where's the gun at you used to killed Deniro?"

"Let me get it."

Jamila came walking through the doors clapping her hands, "that's how you get shit done the right way. You walk up to a mother fucker put the gun to his fucking head and you squeeze that bitch three times. Leaving pieces of his fucking face on the window. That's how you kill a fucking rat. Lorenzo makes sure the cars get burnt."

"Already took care of that. And here is the gun used to kill Deniro."

"Good, I'll hang it up right next to the one used to kill Sammy."

Jamila opened her purse to see that Morwell was calling her. "Lorenzo, hold on a second let me take this call."

"Hello."

144

"I just got done watching the news Jamila and I see our problem has been taken care of. I know I could put my trust in you."

"I glad to know you trust me."

"I see you going very far in this life, I will be in touch Jamila."

.

"I'll be waiting to hear from you."

Hanging up the phone Jamila walked back over to Lorenzo.

"Jamila, I forgot to tell you right before you came in here. I got a call from Cap Deniro. He saw the news and wanted to know if you can come by and see him today."

"I'm not up to meet no one. You can if you want to meet up with him today. Have him meet you at Destiny's. I got some calls to make, I 'll see you in a few."

SAYNOMORE

Chapter Seventeen

"Thank you for coming to see me, Cap."

"No problem Vinnie."

"I remember the first time Tony brought me to the docks. We were standing right here looking at the Hudson. Do you know how many people I dropped off the bridge when Tony was alive? It's no secret that Red Invee and Frankie are allies ever since she came on the scene. Tony first then Sunnie after Sunnie it was Sammy. And the last one was Alex. now I'm the head of the family."

"And how many people been killed in your family Deniro?" asked Cap.

"Johnny and Blue and I still can count on you. You know there will be a choosing for the New Don for the new head of the 7. And Red Invee is going to get that seat. And there is nothing we can do about it; she is too smart for her own good."

"Cap have you ever asked yourself how did all that end up in Deniro's trunk the day he met with Red Invee. Then out the blue the FBI pull him over a few minutes later."

"It was a set up Vinnie, we all know that. But it's not what you know, it's what you can prove that counts. So, you called me out here for what to go over family history of wars?"

"No to hopefully get an Ally, because the enemy of our enemy is our friend. I am your friend, and you make a good point. And you're not the only one who dropped a few bodies in the Hudson. So, what you want to kill Red Invee?"

"You couldn't have said it better, Cap," said Vinnie. "We just need the Scott family on board with us."

"I think I can talk with Jimmy. Give me a few days and I'll let you know something."

Vinnie shook Cap hand and patted him on the back before walking off.

*****

Cap walked in the hotel with four of his men. He met Lorenzo at the front desk.

"Don Cap, thank you for coming by."

"No problem Lorenzo."

"Please you and your guys follow me to the ballroom."

As they sat down at the table a waiter came up and poured them all shots of gin. Lorenzo without being disrespectful, I was hoping to speak with Red Invee.

"She is very busy at the moment. She sends her apologies to you. Don Cap, I asked you to come by here because I really don't know how this war started between our families. You had a few people die and we had a few die as well. I saw on the news today that Mr. Deniro is dead. He was killed on the transporting bus. Don Cap, Red Invee would like to call this war off between our families. No one else has to die," said Lorenzo.

"I would like that very much, it's no point for more lives to be taken for no reason."

"So, we agree this war is over?"

"Yes, I agree Lorenzo. Deniro was wrong for getting involved in Marcus and Frankie's personal business. Now Deniro and Marcus are dead. On the behalf of the Deniro family I would like for you to accept my apology."

"Thank you, Don Cap, I will let Red Invee know." With those words the war was over.

Jamila was watching the news on Deniro's assassination was being ran when Lorenzo walked in her office.

"I see you still watching the story on Deniro."

"I am, I had the meeting with Don Cap, and he agreed the war should have never started. It should have been over, and we are at peace with each other."

"That's good to hear."

"So, what's next?" asked Lorenzo.

"I want to open up a few night clubs and some other businesses up here."

"That sounds like a plan."

"How Morwell taking the good news?"

"He is very pleased with the outcome. Come take a ride with me Lorenzo. I told Frankie I would come talk to Fabio when this is all over. Come on, let's go. I'll have the car pulled around front."

Walking through the doors of Frankie meat market Jamila saw Fabio talking to one of Frankie's men. Fabio looked dead at Jamila, "Excuse me for a minute. Jamila, honestly, I ain't think you was going to come."

"I gave my word I would be here and that's all we have."

"Come have a seat with me over here for a minute."

"Fabio, I don't have a lot of time."

"Jamila, I know what I did was wrong, and I am sorry for it. I love you Jamila and always have. What do I have to do to make thinks right between the two of us?" replied Fabio.

"Fabio, I do love you, but our time ended four years ago when you knew we was at war. And you and Frankie had me believing you was dead. You left me after I killed two people in front of you for you. I will never trust you or Frankie ever again. I thank you for everything, but our season is over, I'm sorry."

Jamila got up and kissed Fabio on the forehead and walked off. Fabio looked at her without saying a word. Lorenzo was outside waiting on her when she walked through the door.

"So where do we go now?" asked Lorenzo.

"Home, we have a lot to deal with and not a lot of time."

"You told him it was over with?"

"Yea, I did," replied Jamila.

"How he takes it?"

"You know what I don't know, and I really don't care."

As the car was pulling off Jamila looked at Fabio through the window knowing she will always love him. But his lies broke the foundation of loyalty they stood on.

*****

"So, what now, Jamila and Frankie are off the case?"

"Yea, I don't like this shit but everything we had on both of them went up in smoke, files, pictures, recordings, everything." Said Chief Tadem.

"So, who you think got Deniro whack?"

"Anybody could put two and two together on that Detective Boatman. It was one of the families that had him killed but shit we can't prove it at all. But one thing I can say like John Gotti and Al Capone, there will be an eight by ten waiting for they ass too. If we don't find them dead in the streets dead with, their eyes open in a pool of blood. One thing I can say Boatman is everyone has their time. We just have to wait until they time is up."

"You know what Chief Tadem. I honestly believe Jamila LaCross is behind this. Everyone who comes across the LaCross family dies. We might have to face the fact that Jamila LaCross might become the first female Don of New York City." said Boatman.

"You might have a point Detective Boatman let me make some calls and I'll get back to you in a little while."

*****

"Fabio slow down with that bottle."

Looking at Frankie, Fabio placed the bottle down on the bar.

"So, you think that's its Frankie?"

"No, she will come around, she just needs sometimes that's it, Fabio. Red Invee heart is very cold when she mad. She done killed more people in four years than I have in ten years. She is very well respected out here."

"I can tell Frankie you think she got Deniro killed?" asked Fabio

"I don't know but I wouldn't put it pass her."

"Fabio, I remember her calling me a few years back asking me for a few men. When I found out she had Alex kidnaped I knew then she was a problem. And how she killed Sammy when me and Chris walked out there to see him lying face down in the mud with three bullet holes in the back of the head. That showed all of us she was about her business," said Frankie.

"So why you think she named her family LaCross?"

"I asked her that, she said one reason was because of your mother and father. She wanted their names to live on. And second reason was to revenge your name besides the blood she spilled over you. She always says the best revenge is massive success."

"I need to go for a ride and clear my head Frankie."

"Fabio you are not in the right state of mind right now to be driving."

Getting up and stumbling two steps back Fabio grabbed a hold of the bar.

"Frankie the war is over. Deniro is dead and Red Invee hates me. I need some air. I'll be at the house later Frankie."

*****

"I'm glad to see you made it Detective Boatman money talks, so you got my attention."

"That's good to hear come on. Mr. Paul Scott is in the back waiting for you now."

"Mr. Scott this is Detective Boatman."

"Detective Boatman, I see you're ready to crossover to the dark side and play in my world."

"Mr. Scott is that what you think? Your world?" replied Boatman with a smile on his face.

"I'm already playing in it."

"So, what can you do for me Detective?"

"That depends on one thing, how much are you paying me?"

"How does $10,000 a month sound?" said Mr. Scott.

Pulling the chair out and taking a seat in front of Mr. Scott's desk.

"I'm thinking more like $15,000 a month."

"How dare you come in my place and try to bully me?"

"You get what you pay for and I'm not bullying you around. Now Jamila LaCross, I'm bullying her around with $20,000 a month. So, $15,000 shouldn't be a problem for you."

"How can I trust you if you work for her?" asked Cap.

"See that's the thing I'm not working for her. Let's just say she hit the wrong ball out the park and I caught it."

"So, you do play in my world Detective. Good then $15,000 I want to know everything and more Detective Boatman. What you hear I hear. what you see I see is that clear enough for you Detective?"

"Just know Don Cap the greater the risk, the higher the payout. I don't work for free what you piss out I don't drink. And what you eat I don't shit. So, I need my money upfront and if you need a job done let me know two days ahead of time and let this be a start of a beautiful friendship. Thanks for the money and I can see my way out walking out the door." Detective Boatman smiled at Don Cap one last time before he was gone.

"You know what I'll step over his dead body one day. I'll burn down his fucking house and kill his fucking kids. I may even burn them alive. I'll keep an eye on him Don Cap."

"Good do that."

*****

"It's closing time and it looks like you still have a lot on your mind Jamila."

"I do Lorenzo. Come over here and have a drink with me. Bring the bottle of Gray Goose."

"You want ice Jamila?"

"No, thanks, now come over here and relax with me."

"Here's your drink. So has Fabio been reaching out to you lately?"

"A few times. He left messages for me to call him back. But I'm not. I done killed with my own hands over twenty-five people for him. Fabio is dead in my eyes no matter how much I love him. Love will get you killed loyalty won't."

"Jamila, loyalty is only as strong as trust."

"Lorenzo trust is only as strong as the foundation you stand on and we stand on foundation of loyalty."

"Yea, yea, yea."

"One more thing Lorenzo."

"And what's that?"

"Checkmate."

"Whatever! What you about to do now Jamila?"

"I might go home and get some rest."

"That sounds like a plan to me."

"I'll see you tomorrow Lorenzo."

"Ok peace Jamila."

Jamila drove around the streets of NY. She pulled into Red Hook projects and was just looking around and she saw Chomorrow aka Man a kid she knew since he was eleven years old. He had a book bag on, so she knew he was a runner from the way he looked and how he was moving. She backed her car up and drove home when she pulled up, she saw a white F-150 parked out front. When she got out her car Fabio stepped out the truck and walked up to her. Without turning around, she pulled her black 9mm out and pointed it at his face, stopping him in his tracks.

"What the fuck are you doing here? How you know where I live?" said Jamila.

"I still have a lot of friends here. Jamila, I came here to talk to you."

"We don't have shit to talk about."

"Can you put the gun down and stop pointing it at me? replied Fabio.

"I should pull the trigger. Give me one reason I shouldn't kill you?"

"I'll give you three. One, if you wanted to kill me, I'll be dead already. Two is because you know I still love you and I'm sorry for what I did and how I hurt you. Three, is because I know you still love me."

Jamila put her gun down. "Fabio, if you love me, respect me and my space and give me the time I asked for and leave me alone until I'm ready to talk."

Fabio looked at Jamila shook his head.

"Jamila, I'll be waiting on you Queen."

Jamila watched as he walked off knowing if Fabio could find her anybody could find her. She put a mental note in her head to move ASAP.

*****

Frankie sat outside his house next to the pool smoking his cigar reading the newspaper when Fabio walked up.

"So, did she talk to you?" asked Frankie.

"No, she put a gun to my head. This is the second time she did this."

Frankie laughed as he pulled on his cigar.

"Fabio, a good coach knows when to expect a loss in a game. My child will come around when she ready."

"Your child?"

"Yea, she is my first black child Fabio, and you are drunk. You need to go lay down for a while."

"Yea, ok." Fabio said as he walked off. Frankie shook his head and continued reading his newspaper.

Chapter Eighteen

The room was quiet with a dim light as 7 families sat around the round table with shot glasses in front of them with brandy poured in them. Frankie stood up and looked around before talking.

"We all know why we are here but, before we start, I would like to take a toast to Tony and Chris the last two Dons of the 7."

Everyone picked up they glasses and said at one time, "To Tony and Chris."

"Families it's been too long that the 7 seats have been empty. It's time for us to pick a new Don. We know the rules, we can't pick ourselves, someone has to choose you."

Cap stood up, "the Lenacci family was the head of the table for years. It's only right that the new Don goes to Vinnie the head of the Lenacci family," with those words he took his seat.

Everyone tapped their shot glasses on the table. Tommy Gunz stood up.

"Frankie Landon is the oldest here. He's been a part of the 7 from the very beginning. He walked with Tony and Chris before half of you was born. He's been in multiple wars and he still stands. Frankie Landon is the only right choice."

Everyone tapped they glasses again.

"I have a choice."

"Mr. Scott who you chose?"

"I chose Red Invee."

Everyone looked at him.

"I know we never had a female Don or a black Don in all the years."

Red Invee watched as he talked.

"Four years ago, she went to war with the Lenacci family because Tony, Sammy, Sunnie down to Alex all tried to make her pay due's. She refused when the rest of us was paying and it cost them, they live. A year and a half ago for no reason Mr. Deniro started a war with her and it cost him big in the end. Red Invee been fair to all of us. When Sammy set all of us up Red Invee saved who she could and killed Sammy that rainy night. When Chris and

Frankie gave her the locket, I was told she ripped the contract up and threw the locket away. She said I did what was right not for a reward and I'm not going to hold nothing over your head. Then just a few days ago word came to me she had Deniro killed when he was going to bring all of us down when none of us could get to him, she did. She's loyal, honest, true and above all she always put the 7 first. She's the one we need as the new Don. Does anybody disagree? If not, I choose Red Invee."

Everybody raised they hands for Jamila to be the new Don. Red Invee was loss for words looking around as the first black female Don, as everyone clapped and took shots in her name.

*****

Red Invee walked in her office and to her surprise Lorenzo had everyone there they started clapping as she walked in the door. Lorenzo yelled to the new Don, the queen of the city Red Invee, Red Invee, everyone yelled.

"Congrats on becoming the new Don."

"Thank you Jatavious."

"How does it feel to be the new Don?"

"I really don't know yet, this is all new to me," said Red Invee.

"A lot of responsibility comes with that position. So, I heard you was the one who had Deniro killed. I was breaking my brain trying to see who done it. I can honestly say you got the job done with no questions asked. I have to make some runs enjoy your party."

"Thank you Jatavious."

Looking at Lorenzo she made her way to the front of the table. He passed her a champagne glass looking at everyone.

"Thank you, Lorenzo! Thank you all for being here today. It's been a long road and now the LaCross family is the head of the family NYC Underground Mafia world. To loyalty, trust, respect, honor, devotion. But this is far from over, it's just the beginning for us. Young boy, Badii, Muscle and Lorenzo. I love you all, no words can express how I feel about you. It's because of you I am now the Queen of New York City and the new Don."

Frankie watched everything from the corner. Red Invee ain't even know he was there. He was proud of her because she came along way. He stood up so she could see him.

"Everyone please enjoys yourselves and thank you all again."

Frankie looked at her as walked up to him. "Congrats Red Invee."

"Thank you, Frankie, I ain't no you were here."

"Yes, Lorenzo called up and asked me to come."

"Where is Fabio?" asked Red Invee

"He had some business back in Paris to take care of. I remember the first time I saw you, now look at you the new Don. You have come a very long way."

"It's because of you helping me along the way Frankie," replied Red Invee

"So, what's next for you now?" asked Frankie

"I have one more thing to take care of then I'll open shop back up."

"And what's that that you need to take care of?"

"It's not important but thank you Frankie for everything."

Red Invee gave Frankie a kiss on the cheek before walking off. Frankie just watched Red Invee as she walked around talking and laughing. It was her day, and she was now his boss.

*****

The black limousine sat under the train tracks it was 9pm that night. You had a few smokers standing around a trash can warming up as the fire came out it. Red Invee had two men outside her limousine with AR15's in their hands, waiting on someone to meet her. She was on the phone with Morwell as she waited. .

"So, tell me Red Invee is this a safe line to talk on?"

"Yes, it is."

"So, you were telling me that someone might be trying to set you up?" ask Morwell.

"From what I was told yes."

"Red Invee you are now the don of NYC, play time is over. You need to make them fear you. To respect you. There are two different types of respect, they respect you, but you need the respect that makes them fear you."

"Morwell hold on. Here he comes now."

"If you don't mind can I hear this conversation?" asked Morwell.

"Sure, I'll put the phone down."

The door opened up and a man got in and sat across from Red Invee.

"I know you," replied Red Invee, "you are a part of the Deniro family. I saw you at the bar there."

"I'm a part of the Deniro family, I'm not a rat nor a snitch but, I will protect my own meaning my wife and kids."

"So, what is it you told Lorenzo that was so important you needed to talk to me about?" asked Red Invee.

"Red Invee you are the new Don and it's only right that I tell you Vinnie and Don Cap are plotting against you. They had a secret meeting a few days ago about you and they were talking about teaming up."

"What's your name?" replied Red Invee

"Tommy Gunz."

"Ok, Tommy Gunz I respect you for coming forward with this information. Call Lorenzo tomorrow around 6pm. I'll have something for you."

"Yes, Ms. LaCross."

Red Invee tapped the window two times and the door opened up to let him out.

"Morwell are you still there?"

"Yes, I am, see Jamila that man respects you as the new Don. But that conversation he was talking about was a few days ago. See that's not the respect you need, let me take care of this for you one time as you took care of Deniro for me."

"What are you going to do?"

"I'll send up Oso there and make a point. And I want you to remember Red Invee. We can't have no heart in this game. You are in the big leagues now and we play for keeps." said Morwell.

"I understand Morwell."

"Good. Oso will see you in a few days be ready when he calls."

"I will be."

Red Invee hung up the phone and tapped the window one more time and the doors opened up. Her guys got in and the limo pulled off.

SAYNOMORE

Chapter Nineteen

It's been three days since Jamila talked to Morwell, she knew she was very respected in NYC but Morwell wanted her to be feared in New York City, a different type of respect. Her thoughts were interrupted by the ringing of her phone.

"Hello, Red Invee it's Oso."

"Hey, Morwell told me you would be calling."

"Yes, I'm in NJ right now off of Patterson at the brink warehouse. Can you come meet me here right away?" asked Oso.

"Sure, I'm on my way, I'll be there in twenty minutes."

"Ok, I'll be waiting on you."

Placing her phone in her purse as she walked out her office doors to the main lobby.

"Mrs. Jackson have my car pulled out front and Nick you're coming with me."

"Nick walked Red Invee to her limo as she was talking to Lorenzo over the phone."

"Yes, I'm on my way to see Oso so I need you at the restaurant. I'm leaving Destiny's right now."

"I'm on my way right now," replied Lorenzo, "and keep me posted on what's going on."

"I will Lorenzo, I'll talk to you when I get back."

"Ok."

When the limo pulled up Nick opened the door for her to get out. Oso had LK at the door waiting on her when she pulled up.

"Red Invee, Oso is waiting on you inside please follow me."

Walking inside the damp warehouse Oso came from the back with no shirt on. You can tell he's been shot because of the long scar on his stomach. He had blood on him with rubber gloves on.

"Red Invee I'm here because Morwell asked me to come. Before you walk through these doors, he told me to tell you, you can't have a heart. Respect is one thing fear is another level of respect. So, are you ready?"

"Yes, I am Oso."

"Come on then, let's put some fear in their hearts." Red Invee walked through the doors and saw Vinnie and Don Cap tied to a chair. LK had a gun to both their heads looking at Oso for the word. Red Invee looked at them.

"I see ya got together for another meeting about me. The two new allies not going the way you planned and Vinnie of all people you."

"Red Invee don't worry about them today, they will pay in blood money for they mistake. LK go bring them out."

Red Invee just watched as LK walked off. She was so confused of who Oso was talking about. Vinnie and Don Cap just looked at Red Invee with pleading eyes. Nick stood next to her with a M16 in his hand. Red Invee watched as LK brought back two females and a boy with bags over the heads. With their hands tied up behind their backs.

"Mr. Vinnie your wrongs against the new Don cost you blood money and look who we got. Oso looked at LK that's when he pulled the bag of his daughter's head. She tried to run to him, but LK pulled her back, dropping her on the floor. He started jumping around in the chair trying to scream. Oso pulled out a machete.

"Vinnie, Ms. LaCross wants blood money for your disloyalty."

Red Invee just watched as tears came from Vinnie's eyes looking at his fifteen-year-old daughter about to die. Vinnie watched now with a smile on his face and one swing her head hit the concrete floor and rolled off some.

"Your mistake cost her, her life. Next time it will be your whole fucking family."

"Don Cap your turn and we got two, let's see who they are."

LK pulled the bags off their heads and it was his wife and son. Vinnie was just looking at his daughter's head on the floor not hearing nothing no one said. Don Cap was trying to say something LK took the rag out his mouth.

"Please don't. Please."

"Mr. Cap, I don't understand that word please. When you were going against the new Don. Look at your beautiful wife and handsome son who are about to die. Now LK, I'm letting you take care of these two."

"Red Invee, please no, stop them. Don't let them do it." LK looked at her.

"LK get me my blood money. Don Cap your actions killed your son and wife. LK kill his son first, I want both his parents to see they child die." Don Cap looked at his nine-year-old son crying as LK cut his throat. His body hit the floor as blood poured out his neck. Red Invee walked up to his wife. "Thank your husband for this pulling her gun out. Don Cap do you have anything to say?"

"No, good."

Pulling the trigger blood went everywhere as her body fell backwards on the floor.

"What you want to do with these two, Red Invee?"

"Cut they pinky fingers off, their right hand and let them go. They know where to find me next time they whole fucking family will die. Oso thank you for your help and tell Morwell I'll be in touch."

Red Invee and Nick walked out the warehouse LK locked the door behind them.

*****

"Mr. Don Cap, I see it in your eyes you want revenge so bad because what you have witnessed today. Your flesh and blood being killed in front of you and there wasn't nothing you could have done to save her life. I know it hurts but this is what happens when you cross the Queen Don. You had to pay in blood money. Now let me tell you this, your mother, little sister and father all live in a brownstone in Brooklyn. And your son who is in college plays football for LSU will all have horrible deaths in a very painful way if you ever cross the Queen Don again."

"And you of all people Vinnie, after she helped you become the head of the Lenacci family and agreed to clean your money. You crossed her so you as well had to pay in blood money, it was the only way to make this right. Now Vinnie your brother and his family of five lives in Deer Park NY, Long Island. And your mother is very sick, and we know she been at Southside hospital for a while now."

"Don't let us pay her a visit because she won't like it. I'm letting you bury your loved ones. LK bring me the three body bags. One more thing before we leave, you must also know pain."

Oso walked behind them with a pair of bolt cutters.

"Mr. Don Cap this is going to hurt. With one cut Don Caps finger hit the floor as he screamed in pain as he saw the blood squirting on the floor."

"Vinnie it's your turn."

"Ahhhh," Vinnie yelled as his finger hit the floor. Picking them up placing them in a bag he looked at LK.

"Cut them loose, they are not stupid. Mr. Morwell sends his love to you, please let's not have this talk again."

Oso looked at them as they were over top of their dead love one's bodies.

"Come on LK it's time for us to go. Now our work here is done."

Chapter Twenty

"Jatavious, you need to talk with Red Invee, she respects you."

"Mr. Scott, it's a beautiful day outside let's take a walk around the city park."

As they walked out the lobby doors heading across the street to the park Mr. Scott had his two men following behind them.

"So, what is the problem that you came to see me about because you said I need to talk with Red Invee?"

"She is becoming too powerful. She's only been the Queen Don for two months and she's running everything with an iron fist."

"You had people riding bikes and walking the dog in the park and sitting on benches as they walked past them."

"Is this conversation about what happened to Vinnie and Don Cap family you are talking about?" asked Jatavious.

"Yes, that's part of it. She had Addy Gambino tied to the train tracks as the train was coming. She was standing there talking to him eating an apple because he was short with her money."

"I heard about that too Mr. Scott. She gave him I believe 30 kilos for $18,000 apiece and he decided to go behind her back and try to go to the source and it got back to her. To my understanding she let him live."

"Yes, she did. They got him up before the train could hit him. But his brother and business partner were killed by the train and she still wanted her money, and she gave him seventy-two hours to get it up." Said Mr. Scott.

"She wanted blood money for the plot to overthrow her. She could have killed they whole family but, she didn't. They ain't respect her enough to let her have the 7 so, she made them respect her with fear and blood. They brought that on themselves. She is paying off police officers for everyone else, judges, DA's for the 7. She is flooding the streets with pure cocaine Mr. Scott. She is becoming the Untouchable but she's putting the 7 first."

"I understand that Mr. Jatavious. She had his daughter's head cut off in front of him. And Don Caps son's throat slit in front of him. Red Invee also shot his wife and killed her too," replied Mr. Scott.

"She did what she needed to do to make them understand who she is now. When Tony was the Don all he did was sit in this club and drink and made everyone pay dues. The only family that matter was the Lenacci family. When Chris took the chair, we never saw him. Both men had one thing in common, they thought they was bigger than the 7 and both men died thinking that. Red Invee put the 7 first. She risked her family killing Deniro's rat ass and when Sammy tried to kill all the heads, she stopped him. Just this conversation could get us both killed if it was brought back to her watered down with lies. Give her a chance, it's new I know, a black female Don, but let's face the facts it's real. I ain't never think I would see it, but I did, now my friend I have a few things to take care of. Let her be, trust in the new Don."

With them words Jatavious walked off leaving Mr. Scott next to his limousine.

*****

"Badii."

"What's up Young Boy?"

"I haven't seen so much blood in all my life. Over these last few months, we been putting bodies in the dumpster and dropping them off behind buildings. Red Invee has no understanding, she has to move like that now that she is the Queen Don of NYC. She doesn't give a fuck who you are she wants you to understand her word is law. You weren't there when she had me and muscle tie them dudes up from the Gambino family. Real shit, I thought we were going to cut them lose. But when I saw the train coming, I knew then shit was real. She had us untie Addy Gambino. When we went to untie his brother, she stopped us and said let them die. After that she told Addy he had seventy-two hours to have her money before walking off back to the limousine. It is what it is that shit is over and done with. Come on we have a job to go take care of. Just look at it this way, was you tied to the train tracks and your pockets are heavy. And like I said, we got a job to do, and she is expecting us to meet her at Jelani's in forty-five minutes so let's get a move on its Fam.

*****

With two guns in his hand Don Cap was walking back and forth thinking how he wanted Red Invee killed in the worst way for what she did to his family. Just knowing she was on the way to see him and everyone else at the meeting for the 7 got under his skin. Seeing his wife and son being killed and there wasn't nothing he could do killed him inside. He knew he was going to kill Red Invee, it was just a matter of time.

"Go get the car it's time to go make sure you have extra clips and tell pain and brick they are coming with us. Today might be the day we kill a nigga Don."

*****

"Jamila, we need to talk."

"About what Lorenzo?"

Taking her red sport jacket off and laying it on the back of her chair. Sitting down at her desk she looked at Lorenzo.

"Jamila you are putting fear in the hearts of the 7. It's like you don't have no understanding no more. This isn't you killing kids and tying people to train tracks. I understand you have to show them you are not to be fucked with but there are other ways to do it."

"Lorenzo, we been tried by the Lenacci family, Deniro family and Scott family. Fabio and Frankie both lied to me for years. I don't give a fuck no more. I'm a black female Don and the head of the Mafia in NYC. I can't let nothing get by me no more. If you try me my actions will be ten times worse than what they thought I would do. People only respect violence and I'll show them how bloody and ruthless I can be if you cross me."

"Lorenzo you remember DA Moore?"

"Yea, the DA who was running your case and Frankie and Deniro's too," replied Lorenzo.

"Did you know he was pushing the DEA and FBI to reopen up the case against us?"

"No, I didn't know that."

"See I do what I do to protect all the families under the 7. Come on before it's too late, I have Badii and Young Boy waiting on us. We are going to the farm for this meeting with the 7 where Sunnie was last alive at. I have a surprise for the families there."

*****

"Frankie what is this place?"

"It's the farm Fabio. I been here before and if we are here then that means someone is going to die."

Fabio looked around at everything from the trees to the people walking around with guns to the other families still sitting in their cars. He even saw wild dogs running around. That's when he saw the black limo pulling up on the dirt road.

"Frankie, she's here."

Everyone stepped out they cars as Red Invee's limo pulled up. Two bodyguards opened her limo door. Young boy and Badii were in the car behind them. Red Invee stepped out the limo walking in her $3,000 red-bottom shoes. She was dressed like a model America's Next Top Model. She walked up to everyone and greeted them with a kiss on the cheek.

"I know you are all wondering why I asked you to come here for the meeting. I asked you all her for two reasons. One is because we have a pest that just won't go away. And two, so we can get a clear understanding on a few things. But first, let's see about this pest that just won't go away."

Red Invee looked at Badii and Young Boy and nodded her head. Everyone looked at him within a few minutes you saw a man with a bag over his head who was beaten and dragged to the front of them.

"So, look at this man, does anybody know who he might be?"

Red Invee looked around at everyone and walked over to him. "I'll show you who he is."

As she pulled the bag off his head she said, "everyone looks at DA Moore the man who wants all of us locked in cells for life or waiting to die on death row. Don't look surprised Mr. Moore. See you have your justice team and I have mine."

"Where am I?"

"You are at the round table of the 7."

"Where is Allen? He was with me last night." said DA Moore as he looked around with blood over his face at everyone standing around looking at him.

"Young Boy go get Allen for him and bring him here." Red Invee walked up to Badii and took the machete he had in his hand and walked back over to DA Moore.

"Frankie you think she's going to kill him?"

"Fabio, I know she is going to kill him and whoever Young Boy brings out here. I told you she is not the same person no more."

"See Mr. Moore, you have the Lenacci family, Landon family, the Scott family, Gambino family, the Deniro family, the Zimmerman family, and the LaCross family. We are the underground lawmakers. Your case blew up and your witness slash snitch I had killed. And you just couldn't leave the case alone. You pushed the issue to reopen it so now here we are."

Red Invee looked to see Young Boy bringing Allen out. Once he was next to DA Moore, he pushed him down on the ground where he fell on his face. Red Invee kneeled where she was face to face with DA Moore. He was looking at her with his hands tied as blood came from his lip.

"Since you can't leave this case alone, I'll have to make sure it's a dead bolt case," said Red Invee.

"You think it's going to stop with me? You kill me and you will have more police on your ass than ever before."

"DA Moore, I've killed cops, judges, FBI agents and still I stand. So, I'll take that chance then I'll go see your wife and children off of Dickson Avenue."

Don Cap looked at Vinnie when she said that Vinnie brushed the look off knowing she meant what she said about killing the rest of his family.

Allen looked at Moore, "This is the way we die. Moore I'll see you on the other side friend." As he spoke those words Red Invee looked at him.

"Allen you will see him on the other side." She swung the machete one hard time and took Allen's head clean off.

DA Moore saw that and started throwing up as he was bent over, she took the machete and slammed it into the back of his head killing him too. She then looked at the 7.

"Does anyone have something to say about me?" replied Red Invee.

"I do what the fuck I do for all of us. I had Deniro killed before he can rat and take us all down. I pay these fucking judges, DA's, and cops so we can move how we move. I don't give a fuck who at this farm don't give a fuck about me, but you will respect me by my will, or my fucking will. And if it's my will, you will not like it. I promise. I have one job to do and that's to ensure the safety of the seven. I don't ask for dues like Tony did and I don't sit in the house on the hill like Chris did. I'm in the city with you. I'm not your enemy and you don't want me as one. Does anybody have anything to say before we leave here today?" asked Red Invee.

"I do."

"And what's that Mr. Scott?"

"How did you know that he was opening the case back up against us?"

"The same way I knew Mr. Deniro was going to be on that bus. I pay my way very well Mr. Scott for our families."

"Anybody else?"

Red Invee looked around at everyone's faces. "Good, I'm glad we all know where I stand at." Red Invee walked back over to Lorenzo.

"Have them put both bodies in a freezer. I don't want the dogs eating at them."

"You want me to keep them here?" asked Lorenzo.

"Yea. Everyone knows what I'm capable of and they don't want to play them deadly games with me, because I play for keeps."

Red Invee walked to her limo as she looked at Frankie and Fabio get into the limo and pulled off.

SAYNOMORE

Chapter Twenty-One

"Detective Boatman, we have a big problem. Last week DA Moore went missing with his driver. We put out an APB on him and Allen. I need you to hit the streets and see what you can come up with."

Looking at Chief Tadem as he smoked his cigarette and leaning back in his chair. "Sir what you think happened to him?" asked Boatman.

"Your guess is as good as mine. But what I do know is that Jamila has taken on the underground name of Red Invee. And that she is the new Don. I also heard that we put two cases on her, and she got through the cracks. She is becoming the untouchable and before we know it, she's going to be too powerful. We need to bring her ass down fast."

"Wait one fucking minute, DA Moore was trying to reopen the case against her? We have a fucking rat in our system. Someone is talking to her and I'm willing to bet she got her hands in this missing person case. You know what, get on this case as of now. Drop everything else you are doing, and I want eyes on her twenty-four hours a day."

"I'm on it."

Detective Boatman walked out the Chief's office singing. "They see me rolling, they are hating, patrolling, they trying to catch me rolling dirty. Trying to catch me rolling dirty." Laughing as he walked out the police station.

*****

Fabio walked inside of the Pay Your Way strip club to see Star dancing on the stage. He stopped in front of the stage and looked at her with a smile on his face as he peeled off three $100 bills and dropped them on the stage. He then walked to the back to the VIP seats and ordered a bottle of Cîroc as he waited for Star to finish her dance on stage. Looking at her he thought about the last time they were together when he brought her to his penthouse in Manhattan and sexed her down. Just thinking about how she couldn't take his dick as he was long stroking her and stretching her walls out had him ready to fuck her on stage in front of everybody. The song ended as she started walking his way.

"What's up stranger? Where you been at?"

"You know how I do. I'm here one minute gone the next," replied Fabio.

"So how long you plan on sticking around this time?"

"I'm here for good Star."

"Damn ok. Because you just left a bitch. She laughed out loud.

"Stop it, what time you are leaving here tonight?"

"Why? You act like you want me to come home with you." Said Star with seductive eyes.

"That don't sound like a bad plan."

"Shit, I can leave now, if you give me a minute."

"Let me just go get my things and I'll meet you outside."

"Sayless, I'm in the red Benz," smacking her on the ass as she walked off. Fabio grabbed his bottle of Cîroc and walked out the strip club to his car and waited for her to come outside. It's been a long time since he broke her off and tonight, he needed that power mouth. Just looking at her walk out the club he knew he was going to try her up once she got in the car. He looked at her once she opened the door.

"Damn Fabio, this how you are riding?"

"Come on this is just the tip of the iceberg baby girl. So, you know D been missing you too."

"I bet. It's been a while, let me say hi to my friend," replied Star.

Fabio looked at star as he licked his lips and pulled his thick long dick out and just looked at Star as she started to suck it. He put his car in drive and let out a deep moan as she was sucking his dick hard making popping noises.

"Damn you keep sucking my dick like this I'ma nut all in your mouth," said Fabio.

"That's what I want daddy, let me get what I've been missing."

"Fuck a telly, I need this pussy now." Fabio pulled over behind an abandoned building. "Fuck this get out."

174

Walking around to the back of the car he grabbed her.

"Ready for this dick?"

Biting her bottom lip, she nodded her head looking at Fabio as he turned her around pushing her down on the back of the car.

"Damn daddy my pussy jumping right now."

Dropping his pants, he rammed his dick hard in her wet pussy.

"Ohhhh you are breaking my pussy daddy, you too deep."

"Damn this is what the fuck you wanted right?" Grabbing her waist as he smacked her ass.

"Don't run from this dick."

"Baby pull back just a little, I feel you in my stomach." Grabbing her harder ramming his dick in her back-to-back, Star's legs started to give out on her. Fabio started grinding his hips as Star started creaming all over his dick.

"Shit, I'm about to nut." Turning around, Star dropped to her knees.

"Open your mouth baby, suck this dick."

Looking up at Fabio as he nutted all in her mouth.

"Damn Star, come on you are staying at my house tonight."

SAYNOMORE

Chapter Twenty-Two

It was 8 am that next morning. It was damp outside with a cold chill. Jamila pulled up at the cemetery with a dozen roses. The last time she came to see her father was five years ago. She laid the rose down next to his head stone as tears started pouring down her eyes. She laid a blanket down and knelt on it. She wiped her tears one more time before she started to talk "Dad who have I become? I'm not the same person no more. I have killed so many people in the past six years over love, hate and disloyalty. My friends are dead, one by my own hands and the other I still have nightmares about. I still have nightmares from the time you got tortured, killed and beat in front of me. I want to kill those men so bad dad but, I don't know who they are. And it's eating me up so bad inside I haven't talked to mom in so many years. I just wish you were here, I miss you so, so much dad. I'm the head of my own Mob family called the LaCross. We are one of the strongest families in New York City now. Still to this day, I read the books you gave me and study them. Dad I just don't know what to do no more. Someone I loved with all my heart lied to me and left me when I needed him the most. So how can I let him back into my life? How can I trust him again? What would you do? Your own friend set you up and I don't want that to happen to me again. I had a friend named Nayana and she let love come between us and it got her killed and almost got me killed too. I'm just ready to give up and throw the towel in. I have more than enough money to just run away and never look back. Dad, I just wish you was here with me. I love you and miss you so, so much. Why am I living this life? Can you tell me dad, can you?"

"Excuse me, are you ok?"

"Yes, I am."

"Do you want a tissue?"

"Please, can I have one?"

"Here you go."

"Thank you!"

"So, you know Anthony?"

"Yes, he is my father. How do you know him?"

"We go way back. I knew your father for over forty years, he made a big impact in my life."

"What is your name?" asked Jamila.

"Stephen."

Stephen my name is…"

"Jamila," she cut her off.

"How you know me?"

"I remember when you were a little girl with a cute little puppy walking around with her in your arms everywhere you went."

"So, what's wrong little angel?" replied Stephen.

"My father used to call me that."

"I know, do you want to go get something to eat?"

"Sure, let me just pick up my blanket. My car is the white one over there."

"I'll be right there."

"Ok."

"So where would you like to go eat at?"

"It doesn't matter to me, wherever you want to go."

They pulled up at the Olive Garden.

"So, tell me Jamila, what's wrong?"

"I have done a lot of things in my life that I wish I could take back, but I can't and it's to the point I can't trust no one. I have to stay looking over my shoulders. I know my day is coming, I just don't know when."

"I remember having the same talk with your father. Baby when you feel like giving up just remember why you fought so hard in the first place. Remember the plane takes off against the wind, not with it. Look what you've done for the streets of New York City. You know who I am?" said Jamila.

"Not at first but looking at you I remember your face on the news and all the positive things you been doing."

"Let the news tell it, I'm just another cold-hearted killer running a black Mafia family."

"Sometimes you have to throw the rock in the water to get a chain reaction. Jamila, I'm leaving you with this. Before I go sweet pea. Jesus died on the cross for our sins. The greatest gift in the world. But everyone doesn't see the sacrifice that he did for all of us with that being said, it doesn't matter who you are there is always going to be someone who just don't like you. So just keep rising to the top baby. You have a blessed day and thank you for the lunch."

"You're welcome, do you have a number?"

"If it is meant to be, we will cross paths again."

Just like that Stephen walked out the doors. Jamila sat there for another hour just thinking about what her and Stephen talked about knowing she was right. She paid the bill and went to her car and drove off. She called Lorenzo.

"Hello, hey look meet me at Jelani's in twenty minutes."

"I'm already here," replied Lorenzo.

"Ok, I'll be there in a few."

"I'll see you when you get here."

*****

"So, let's get to the point of this meeting. Look around Mr. Zimmerman, what do you see?"

"I see a room full of people, with the up most respect Mr. Jatavious. What can I do for you?"

"Maybe we can help each other out."

Jatavious walked around the office and took a seat crossing his legs next to Mr. Zimmerman.

"I have friends in high places and to my understanding Ms. LaCross is about to open up a casino in NYC. She already made her way to the top of the food chain. Two wars within six years with two powerful families and she won, Mr. Zimmerman."

"Now you said you see a room full of people let me introduce them to you. To the right you have Mr. Woods and his business partner Mr. Tillman. Over to the left you have Mr. Owen. Now this is what they are willing to do for you. 35% of the casino and let you run it the way you want. Hire who you want, fire who you want too."

"And what's the catch to all of this Mr. Stone?"

"You don't mind if I smoke do you Mr. Zimmerman?"

"No, it's your office."

"Here's the thing. Red Invee is getting too powerful. Soon she will be the Untouchable and before that happens, we need her to disappear." Pulling his cigar and looking at Mr. Zimmerman for his answer.

"What you are asking me to do is treason and it can cost me my life. Just like a conversation as this one cost Vinnie and Don Cap their families and fingers."

"See that's the thing, I'm not Vinnie and you are not Don Cap. I'm Jatavious Stone and my friend you are Kevin Zimmerman. You have one of the strongest families in the city whose ties go all the way to Las Vegas."

"And what insurance do I have?" asked Zimmerman.

Jatavious pulled out a locket with his blood in it and slid a folded-up piece of paper to Mr. Zimmerman with his name on it looking at it.

"You're signing your life over to me."

"No, I'm just in your debt right now."

"What's my window?"

"You have three months and Mr. Zimmerman if word gets out about this it will be your life I'll take, so kill the bitch and become a very rich and powerful man. I'm still a little upset Tony, Sammy, Alex and Carlito were killed, they were all my friends. So now we are asking you to cut the head off and watch the body drop. Let's just put it out there the Lenacci family and Deniro family can't hold a match to the Zimmerman family."

"Mr. Stone, I don't need you putting a battery in my back. I'll have the bitch killed and remember I hold the locket with your blood in it."

Mr. Stone put out his hand and Mr. Zimmerman shook it with a smile on his face. "Kill the bitch."

"She's already dead," was the last words Mr. Zimmerman said as he got up and walked out the office.

*****

Jamila walked into her office to see Lorenzo watching the news on the 72-inch flat screen hanging on the wall.

"What's the news talking about now?"

"The disappearance of DA Moore and his driver Allen. They're asking if anybody have any information on their whereabouts to please call 1800 Crime stoppers," replied Lorenzo.

"You know what, that was what I wanted to talk to you about," said Jamila. "I think it's about time we drop off the dead."

"And where do you want them dropped off at?"

"Where else, the courthouse. Put a sign around DA Moore's neck that say hint hint, stop playing with me."

"And when you want this done?" asked Lorenzo.

"Tonight."

"Let me get on that right now. I'll reach out to you once it's done."

"I'll be waiting to hear from you.:

Watching Lorenzo walk out the office, Jamila looked at the news and saw pictures of DA Moore with the crime stopper number next to his picture. *Sometimes you can't put a bell around a cat's neck you just have to kill him,* Jamila said to herself as she cut the TV off and walked to her private office.

*****

Detective Boatman watched as a local drug dealer named Wordman make a sale from his 2003 black Lexus on the side of Fruit Tree. He got out the car and started walking his way.

"I see the look in your eyes don't fucking do it."

"Fuck," Detective Boatman said as he took off after him.

"I'm going to fuck you up when I catch you."

Watching the man jump the fence down a dark alley over the fence. He went with him running full speed. That's when Detective Boatman pulled his gun out and shot two times at him dropping him after he got hit in the leg.

"What the fuck you shot me man?"

"You think I give a fuck about shooting you?" said Boatman. "You got me running down this dirty ass fucking alley. I should kill your motherfuckin' ass. Now I'm asking you some fucking questions and you're going to give me some fucking answer."

"I ain't telling you shit."

"How you want to fucking die that what it is? You want to die, or you want to talk?"

"Man, what the fuck you want to know?"

"What you know about DA Moore's disappearance?"

"I don't know shit about DA Moore's disappearance."

"I think you fucking lying, I'm asking you one more fucking time. What do you know about DA Moore's disappearance?"

"Tell me what I want to know, or I'll put a bullet in your fucking head, Wordman."

"Shit man everyone knows that Red Invee had his ass knocked off for trying to re-open back up the case against the Mob. What the fuck you are a detective and you ain't know that shit?"

"Now come on man I need to get to the hospital. I'm bleeding out bad man".

"Let me take a look at that leg. Yea, it is pretty bad, I don't think we going to make it to the hospital with that leg, let me see what I can do."

Looking around Detective Boatman made sure no one was around. He pulled his gun out and looked at Wordman.

"Man, what the fuck you are doing?" asked Wordman

"Man, you a rat ain't nobody going to miss you."

"Man don't do this."

With three pulls of the trigger, Wordman was shot dead in the head. "Fucking rat," detective Boatman said as he walked away.

*****

"Badii and Young Boy listen, make sure you have gloves on. We don't need no slip ups at all. We don't need no DNA dropped on these bodies."

"So, where are we dropping them off?"

"The courthouse, Badii."

"Yo, that shits crazy Lorenzo."

"Young Boy, let's just get this shit done. They are stiff they been in the freezer for thirty days."

"Yo, Red Invee don't fucking play at all Lorenzo."

"The Mayor, cops, FBI agents, DA's, rats, when she pushes the button your ass is dead rocker by baby. Badii she plays for keeps. She killed her best friend because she broke her loyalty. She's not to be fucked with. Remember Elisha, he's dead over a secret he kept from her for four years. He's really the reason how our family started. Now he's dead so don't think because ya put in work. She won't kill ya because if you fuck up ya ass will be tied to a tree too. Look when we pull up Young boy open the side door. Badii you are the look out. Young boy we're going to do this real fast and easy lay them down on the steps. Put this note around DA Moore's neck and we are gone." Once they pulled up, they dropped the bodies off Badii looked out for them, they were in and out in less than five minutes.

"Damn she left that boy's head in two piece and took the other dudes head off."

"I told you Young Boy, she plays for keeps. Both of ya listen up, there was a camera in front of the building, so we need this van burned now. So ya take care of it and meet me back at the waste plant tomorrow around 2:30 pm."

"We got you Lorenzo."

"Good, Badii."

Lorenzo opened the van and got out and walked to his car as they drove off.

*****

Local News cameras were everywhere as they took pictures of DA Moore's and his driver Allen's bodies as they laid on the stairs of the NYC courthouse.

"You have to be fucking kidding me. You're telling me that someone just dropped their bodies off. Allen's missing his fucking head from his body and DA Moore's head is cut in two with a fucking note. *Hint, Hint, don't fucking play with me* and nobody saw shit. I want these fucking video cameras reviewed now. And where the fuck is CSI at? I called for them a fucking hour ago."

"Chief Tadem."

"What is it officer?"

"We found the van they drove; it's burnt."

"That's all the fuck I needed to hear bad news on top of worst fucking news. Does anybody get some fucking good news for me today, shit anybody?"

"Who the hell kills a DA and drops their body off at the fucking courthouse?"

"I can't do this right now, I just can't. Ok, listen up, I want my crime scene cleared out and a full report on my desk within the next two hours."

"Chief Tadem, Chief Tadem, can I have a word with you?"

"Sure."

"Can you tell us what the city of NY is doing about all these homicides?"

"And now that DA Moore and his driver's bodies just came up, what are the steps that NYC police are taking on to resolve this crime wave?"

"At this time, we are looking into all major crime families. This is an ongoing investigation, and it will be resolved at the end of this investigation with the arrests of the criminals behind DA Moore's killing and his driver."

Jamila watched the news cast as Chief Tadem did his interview talking about the ongoing investigation. She just hopes she ain't have to have him killed but, she was thinking about paying him a visit at home looking at him talk and giving him a choice "Life or death."

She cut the TV off and turned on the CD player to listen to 50 Cents, *When It Rains, It Pours.*

*****

"Anthony, she is beautiful, smart, bold and looks just like you. Baby I wanted to tell her so bad I'm her Grandmother. The last time I saw her she was only six years old. Baby I can't open up my heart to her knowing she's living the same life you were living, and death is waiting on her too just like he waited on you baby and took you away from me. Mommy loves you so much and it still hurts me every day that you are gone from me. And Symone looks just like her mother, she is getting so big now. When the time is right, I will let them both know I'm their grandmother. I don't know if they know about each other, but faith always has a way of working things out. I love you baby, but mommy has to go now kisses and hugs. Happy 48th birthday."

Stephanie laid the two roses down next to his headstone and kissed her two fingers and touched his headstone before walking away.

*****

"Chief Tadem, here is the report you asked for on DA Moore and Allen Wright."

"Thank you, Jackie."

"Also, I have the autopsy report back on both DA Moore and Allen right."

"Good, read it out to me."

"Wright's cause of death was his head being decapitated and DA Moore suffered a deadly blow to the back of his head. Both bodies were kept in a freezer to the day they were dropped off on the courthouse steps. Now CSI searched both the bodies and found nothing not a single drop of DNA or hair was found on them."

"Thank you, Jackie."

"You're welcome sir, here is the report."

Chief Tadem took the report and walked off to his office closing the door behind him dropping both files on his desk. He pulled out his box of cigarettes and took one out and lite it.

Talking to himself, "Moore what the fuck happened? How did you get caught slipping?" Pulling on his cigarette glancing over the report briefly looking at his wall where he had everyone who was killed over the last six years. He had the officers and people of the law on the right side and the law breakers on the left side. He had pictures of Mayor Oakland at the top on the right side of the wall. And on the left side he had Tony Lenacci on the top and from the top to the bottom he had the most powerful Mafia families in NYC with the LaCross family at the top of it with a picture of Jamila talking with Frankie Landon outside of Chris Scott's funeral. He had a gut feeling that she was behind a lot of these homicide in NYC the questions he asked himself was who she had on her payroll and who could he trust. There was a leak, and he was going to find it.

*****

Fabio walked out of his brownstone to see Detective Boatman leaning against his car smoking a cigarette.

"Do you mind getting off of my car?"

"My bad I was just wondering how it feels to drive one of these $60,000 cars. My car over there ain't cost me more than $5,000 at the police auctions."

"If you don't mind detective, I have some place to be."

"See that's the thing Fabio, I do mind. So, I need you to take five minutes out of your time and hear what the fuck I have to say."

Detective Boatman took one more pull of his cigarette before he flicked it to the ground.

"I remember a few years back you ran Queens and then I heard you stepped on the wrong toes and got your team killed. You faked your death and went into hiding. See I step on the wrong toes every day, but you see this badge right here. That's the keys to the city. And you see this glock on my hip," detective Boatman said as he patted his gun. "This bitch gives motherfuckers act right so, I need you to act right motherfucker. Because you don't want to talk to this bitch, it's going to be a dead conversation."

"What the fuck you want from me man?" replied Fabio.

"See this bitch on my hip had a talk with Wordman and he told her that Red Invee had DA Moore killed."

"I don't know shit about no fucking murder and what the fuck that got to do with me?"

"I'll break this down like ABC and 123, from here on out you going to let me know what the fuck is going on or you and Wordman are going to have a lot in common. When ya two are talking about how this black bitch on my hip gave you both the kiss of death. I'll be in touch real soon chump, and when I do have that input for me."

*****

Chief Tadem walked out his office closing and locking his door behind him. He had his brief case in his hand with the case files on the crime families in NYC.

"Chief Tadem, are you leaving for the night?"

"Yes, Jackie my day went from bad to worst. What's next me having a fucking nightmare?"

"Things will get better in the morning Chief."

"Yea let's see how much better you have a good night Jackie."

"You too sir."

Walking off to Detective Boatman's office he opens the door and saw Boatman at his desk looking on his computer.

"What you are looking at?" asked Chief Tadem

"Strip clubs after hours, you know a lot of crime families do business in night clubs. I'm just trying to get a jump ahead on them."

"Ok, well I'm leaving for tonight take care Boatman."

"See you tomorrow Cheif."

Walking outside to his 1998 Honda he placed his briefcase in the backseat and drove off looking around at the city of New York, which he loved so much. Stopping at the red light he looked around and pulled his box of cigarettes out and lite one up taking a long pull before driving off. Listening to the radio station, they were talking about DA Moore's body being found in the front of the courthouse with a note around his neck. Just listening to them talk about it pissed him off to the max.

Throwing his cigarette out the window he pulled up to his house where his wife and kids were fast asleep. It was 11:30 pm when he walked into his side door. Laying his briefcase down on the kitchen counter with his car keys he opened his refrigerator and pulled out a Coors light. Popping the top open he took a sip and walked in his living room where it was dark at.

"What the fuck," he said as he dropped his beer on the floor looking at Red Invee sitting in his chair looking at him.

He looked to the left and saw his wife and daughters on the love seat as Badii and Young Boy had two guns out looking dead at him. Red Invee looked at him and got up.

"I'm glad to see you are home, Chief Tadem. We need to talk. Don't worry your family is fine and don't be brave and get yourself killed."

Chief Tadem looked at his wife as she looked back at him. She had both of his daughters in her arms asleep on the love seat.

"Cheif Anthony Red, I really hate that it had come to this but, here's the thing you are starting to become a pain in my ass. Some cases are meant to be closed and some doors are not to be walked through. Do you think I wanted to come to your house at this night and hour?"

Chief Tadem ain't say a word, he just looked at Red Invee as she talked.

"You are a smart man so please read between the lines."

Red Invee snapped her fingers and Badii walked up with a bag in his hand and gave it to Red Invee.

"In this bag is $200,000. I'm asking you to just leave it alone and let the dead rest in peace."

Red Invee handed the bag over to Chief Tadem as he took it looking at her and still not talking.

"Your wife is very beautiful and brave. Your daughters are adorable too. Don't be stupid and try to have me locked up for this visit because just like I found you here, someone else will find you for me. And you will not like the outcome. Have a nice day Anthony."

Red Invee snapped her fingers and Badii and Young Boy walked out the house with her. Once there were gone Chief Tadem dropped the bag and ran to his wife.

"Baby, are you ok? Did they hurt you?"

"No, no I was so scared they was going to kill me. Baby I was."

"Don't worry I'm home now, she's not going to get away with this."

"Anthony are you fucking crazy? Please just leave it alone. She could have killed us please." Holding his wife in his arms he kissed her forehead.

"Ok, ok I'll leave it alone."

*****

"So, what now Red Invee?"

"We move forward Badii and hope Chief Tadem plays ball the right way or he will be on the next person on the news with his head missing."

To Be Continued...

Mob Ties 3
Coming Soon

Submission Guideline

Submit the first three chapters of your completed manuscript to ldpsubmissions@gmail.com, subject line: Your book's title. The manuscript must be in a .doc file and sent as an attachment. Document should be in Times New Roman, double spaced and in size 12 font. Also, provide your synopsis and full contact information. If sending multiple submissions, they must each be in a separate email.

Have a story but no way to send it electronically? You can still submit to LDP/Ca$h Presents. Send in the first three chapters, written or typed, of your completed manuscript to:

LDP: Submissions Dept
Po Box 944
Stockbridge, Ga 30281

DO NOT send original manuscript. Must be a duplicate.

Provide your synopsis and a cover letter containing your full contact information.

Thanks for considering LDP and Ca$h Presents.

<u>Coming Soon from Lock Down Publications/Ca$h Presents</u>

BOW DOWN TO MY GANGSTA

By **Ca$h**

TORN BETWEEN TWO

By **Coffee**

THE STREETS STAINED MY SOUL **II**

By **Marcellus Allen**

BLOOD OF A BOSS **VI**

SHADOWS OF THE GAME II

TRAP BASTARD II

By **Askari**

LOYAL TO THE GAME **IV**

By **T.J. & Jelissa**

IF LOVING YOU IS WRONG… **III**

By **Jelissa**

TRUE SAVAGE **VIII**

MIDNIGHT CARTEL IV

DOPE BOY MAGIC IV

CITY OF KINGZ III

By **Chris Green**

BLAST FOR ME **III**

A SAVAGE DOPEBOY III

CUTTHROAT MAFIA III

DUFFLE BAG CARTEL VI

HEARTLESS GOON VI

By **Ghost**

SAYNOMORE

A HUSTLER'S DECEIT III

KILL ZONE **II**

BAE BELONGS TO ME III

A DOPE BOY'S QUEEN III

By **Aryanna**

COKE KINGS V

KING OF THE TRAP III

By **T.J. Edwards**

GORILLAZ IN THE BAY V

3X KRAZY III

De'Kari

THE STREETS ARE CALLING II

Duquie Wilson

KINGPIN KILLAZ IV

STREET KINGS III

PAID IN BLOOD III

CARTEL KILLAZ IV

DOPE GODS III

Hood Rich

SINS OF A HUSTLA II

ASAD

KINGZ OF THE GAME VI

Playa Ray

SLAUGHTER GANG IV

RUTHLESS HEART IV

By Willie Slaughter

FUK SHYT II

By Blakk Diamond

TRAP QUEEN

RICH $AVAGE II

By Troublesome

YAYO V

GHOST MOB II

Stilloan Robinson

CREAM III

By Yolanda Moore

SON OF A DOPE FIEND III

HEAVEN GOT A GHETTO II

By Renta

FOREVER GANGSTA II

GLOCKS ON SATIN SHEETS III

By Adrian Dulan

LOYALTY AIN'T PROMISED III

By Keith Williams

THE PRICE YOU PAY FOR LOVE III

By Destiny Skai

I'M NOTHING WITHOUT HIS LOVE II

SINS OF A THUG II

By Monet Dragun

LIFE OF A SAVAGE IV

MURDA SEASON IV

GANGLAND CARTEL IV

CHI'RAQ GANGSTAS IV

KILLERS ON ELM STREET III

SAYNOMORE

JACK BOYZ N DA BRONX II

A DOPEBOY'S DREAM II

By **Romell Tukes**

QUIET MONEY IV

EXTENDED CLIP III

THUG LIFE IV

By **Trai'Quan**

THE STREETS MADE ME III

By **Larry D. Wright**

IF YOU CROSS ME ONCE II

ANGEL III

By **Anthony Fields**

FRIEND OR FOE III

By **Mimi**

SAVAGE STORMS III

By **Meesha**

BLOOD ON THE MONEY III

By J-Blunt

THE STREETS WILL NEVER CLOSE II

By K'ajji

NIGHTMARES OF A HUSTLA III

By King Dream

IN THE ARM OF HIS BOSS

By Jamila

MONEY, MURDER & MEMORIES III

Malik D. Rice

CONCRETE KILLAZ II

194

Mob Ties 2

By Kingpen
HARD AND RUTHLESS II
By Von Wiley Hall
LEVELS TO THIS SHYT II
By Ah'Million
MOB TIES III
By SayNoMore
BODYMORE MURDERLAND II
By Delmont Player
THE LAST OF THE OGS III
Tranay Adams
FOR THE LOVE OF A BOSS II
By C. D. Blue

Available Now

RESTRAINING ORDER **I & II**
By **CA$H & Coffee**
LOVE KNOWS NO BOUNDARIES **I II & III**
By **Coffee**
RAISED AS A GOON I, II, III & IV
BRED BY THE SLUMS I, II, III
BLAST FOR ME I & II
ROTTEN TO THE CORE I II III
A BRONX TALE I, II, III

SAYNOMORE

DUFFLE BAG CARTEL I II III IV V

HEARTLESS GOON I II III IV V

A SAVAGE DOPEBOY I II

DRUG LORDS I II III

CUTTHROAT MAFIA I II

By **Ghost**

LAY IT DOWN **I & II**

LAST OF A DYING BREED I II

BLOOD STAINS OF A SHOTTA I & II III

By **Jamaica**

LOYAL TO THE GAME I II III

LIFE OF SIN I, II III

By **TJ & Jelissa**

BLOODY COMMAS I & II

SKI MASK CARTEL I II & III

KING OF NEW YORK I II,III IV V

RISE TO POWER I II III

COKE KINGS I II III IV

BORN HEARTLESS I II III IV

KING OF THE TRAP I II

By **T.J. Edwards**

IF LOVING HIM IS WRONG…I & II

LOVE ME EVEN WHEN IT HURTS I II III

By **Jelissa**

WHEN THE STREETS CLAP BACK I & II III

THE HEART OF A SAVAGE I II III

By **Jibril Williams**

A DISTINGUISHED THUG STOLE MY HEART I II & III

LOVE SHOULDN'T HURT I II III IV

RENEGADE BOYS I II III IV

PAID IN KARMA I II III

SAVAGE STORMS I II

By **Meesha**

A GANGSTER'S CODE I &, II III

A GANGSTER'S SYN I II III

THE SAVAGE LIFE I II III

CHAINED TO THE STREETS I II III

BLOOD ON THE MONEY I II

By J-Blunt

PUSH IT TO THE LIMIT

By **Bre' Hayes**

BLOOD OF A BOSS **I, II, III, IV, V**

SHADOWS OF THE GAME

TRAP BASTARD

By **Askari**

THE STREETS BLEED MURDER **I, II & III**

THE HEART OF A GANGSTA I II& III

By **Jerry Jackson**

CUM FOR ME I II III IV V VI VII

An **LDP Erotica Collaboration**

BRIDE OF A HUSTLA **I II & II**

THE FETTI GIRLS **I, II& III**

CORRUPTED BY A GANGSTA I, II III, IV

BLINDED BY HIS LOVE

SAYNOMORE

THE PRICE YOU PAY FOR LOVE I II

DOPE GIRL MAGIC I II III

By **Destiny Skai**

WHEN A GOOD GIRL GOES BAD

By **Adrienne**

THE COST OF LOYALTY I II III

By Kweli

A GANGSTER'S REVENGE **I II III & IV**

THE BOSS MAN'S DAUGHTERS I II III IV V

A SAVAGE LOVE **I & II**

BAE BELONGS TO ME I II

A HUSTLER'S DECEIT I, II, III

WHAT BAD BITCHES DO I, II, III

SOUL OF A MONSTER I II III

KILL ZONE

A DOPE BOY'S QUEEN I II

By **Aryanna**

A KINGPIN'S AMBITON

A KINGPIN'S AMBITION **II**

I MURDER FOR THE DOUGH

By **Ambitious**

TRUE SAVAGE I II III IV V VI VII

DOPE BOY MAGIC I, II, III

MIDNIGHT CARTEL I II III

CITY OF KINGZ I II

By **Chris Green**

A DOPEBOY'S PRAYER

By **Eddie "Wolf" Lee**

THE KING CARTEL **I, II & III**

By **Frank Gresham**

THESE NIGGAS AIN'T LOYAL **I, II & III**

By **Nikki Tee**

GANGSTA SHYT **I II &III**

By **CATO**

THE ULTIMATE BETRAYAL

By **Phoenix**

BOSS'N UP **I , II & III**

By **Royal Nicole**

I LOVE YOU TO DEATH

By Destiny J

I RIDE FOR MY HITTA

I STILL RIDE FOR MY HITTA

By **Misty Holt**

LOVE & CHASIN' PAPER

By **Qay Crockett**

TO DIE IN VAIN

SINS OF A HUSTLA

By **ASAD**

BROOKLYN HUSTLAZ

By **Boogsy Morina**

BROOKLYN ON LOCK I & II

By **Sonovia**

GANGSTA CITY

By **Teddy Duke**

SAYNOMORE

A DRUG KING AND HIS DIAMOND I & II III

A DOPEMAN'S RICHES

HER MAN, MINE'S TOO I, II

CASH MONEY HO'S

THE WIFEY I USED TO BE I II

By Nicole Goosby

TRAPHOUSE KING **I II & III**

KINGPIN KILLAZ I II III

STREET KINGS I II

PAID IN BLOOD **I II**

CARTEL KILLAZ I II III

DOPE GODS I II

By **Hood Rich**

LIPSTICK KILLAH **I, II, III**

CRIME OF PASSION I II & III

FRIEND OR FOE I II

By **Mimi**

STEADY MOBBN' **I, II, III**

THE STREETS STAINED MY SOUL

By **Marcellus Allen**

WHO SHOT YA **I, II, III**

SON OF A DOPE FIEND I II

HEAVEN GOT A GHETTO

Renta

GORILLAZ IN THE BAY **I II III IV**

TEARS OF A GANGSTA I II

3X KRAZY I II

DE'KARI

TRIGGADALE I II III

Elijah R. Freeman

GOD BLESS THE TRAPPERS I, II, III

THESE SCANDALOUS STREETS I, II, III

FEAR MY GANGSTA I, II, III IV, V

THESE STREETS DON'T LOVE NOBODY I, II

BURY ME A G I, II, III, IV, V

A GANGSTA'S EMPIRE I, II, III, IV

THE DOPEMAN'S BODYGAURD I II

THE REALEST KILLAZ I II III

THE LAST OF THE OGS I II

Tranay Adams

THE STREETS ARE CALLING

Duquie Wilson

MARRIED TO A BOSS... I II III

By Destiny Skai & Chris Green

KINGZ OF THE GAME I II III IV V

Playa Ray

SLAUGHTER GANG I II III

RUTHLESS HEART I II III

By Willie Slaughter

FUK SHYT

By Blakk Diamond

DON'T F#CK WITH MY HEART I II

By Linnea

ADDICTED TO THE DRAMA I II III

SAYNOMORE

IN THE ARM OF HIS BOSS II

By Jamila

YAYO I II III IV

A SHOOTER'S AMBITION I II

By S. Allen

TRAP GOD I II III

RICH $AVAGE

By Troublesome

FOREVER GANGSTA

GLOCKS ON SATIN SHEETS I II

By Adrian Dulan

TOE TAGZ I II III

LEVELS TO THIS SHYT

By Ah'Million

KINGPIN DREAMS I II III

By Paper Boi Rari

CONFESSIONS OF A GANGSTA I II III

By Nicholas Lock

I'M NOTHING WITHOUT HIS LOVE

SINS OF A THUG

By Monet Dragun

CAUGHT UP IN THE LIFE I II III

By Robert Baptiste

NEW TO THE GAME I II III

MONEY, MURDER & MEMORIES I II

By **Malik D. Rice**

LIFE OF A SAVAGE I II III

A GANGSTA'S QUR'AN I II III

MURDA SEASON I II III

GANGLAND CARTEL I II III

CHI'RAQ GANGSTAS I II III

KILLERS ON ELM STREET I II

JACK BOYZ N DA BRONX

A DOPEBOY'S DREAM

By **Romell Tukes**

LOYALTY AIN'T PROMISED I II

By Keith Williams

QUIET MONEY I II III

THUG LIFE I II III

EXTENDED CLIP I II

By **Trai'Quan**

THE STREETS MADE ME I II

By **Larry D. Wright**

THE ULTIMATE SACRIFICE I, II, III, IV, V, VI

KHADIFI

IF YOU CROSS ME ONCE

ANGEL I II

By **Anthony Fields**

THE LIFE OF A HOOD STAR

By Ca$h & Rashia Wilson

THE STREETS WILL NEVER CLOSE

By K'ajji

CREAM I II

SAYNOMORE

By Yolanda Moore

NIGHTMARES OF A HUSTLA I II

By King Dream

CONCRETE KILLAZ

By Kingpen

HARD AND RUTHLESS

By Von Wiley Hall

GHOST MOB II

Stilloan Robinson

MOB TIES I II

By SayNoMore

BODYMORE MURDERLAND

By Delmont Player

FOR THE LOVE OF A BOSS

By C. D. Blue

BOOKS BY LDP'S CEO, CA$H

TRUST IN NO MAN

TRUST IN NO MAN 2

TRUST IN NO MAN 3

BONDED BY BLOOD

SHORTY GOT A THUG

THUGS CRY

THUGS CRY 2

THUGS CRY 3

TRUST NO BITCH

TRUST NO BITCH 2

TRUST NO BITCH 3

TIL MY CASKET DROPS

RESTRAINING ORDER

RESTRAINING ORDER 2

IN LOVE WITH A CONVICT

LIFE OF A HOOD STAR

SAYNOMORE

CPSIA information can be obtained
at www.ICGtesting.com
Printed in the USA
LVHW011921170621
690501LV00013B/1290